Duet des Fleurs
and other short distractions

LJ Farrow

Contents

Duet des Fleurs

1

The dream is always the same. It never varies in its dreadfulness, but one doesn't expect a dream about the dreamer's own slow, agonizing death to be anything else. Thankfully, said death never arrives within the dream, for it is always vanquished by my abrupt and anguished waking in the quiet, bubbling hum of my biome tank.

No, I only must endure the seemingly endless fight for oxygen, my muscles screaming at its deficit, my struggles to survive under conditions hostile to an amphibious humanoid. A battle where I, frequently heralded for my strength and resilience, can only watch as the sea ebbs away at low tide. It is the only home I have ever known, receding out of reach. I suffer through airless gasps, like the goldfish that occasionally escape their bowls.

Here in this lab, in the ocean depths of the sunlight zone, the fish and I are adaptive captives, surviving only meters away from real freedom, from the ocean outside. If that world ever encroached on this engineered biodome, this lesser blue marble, we are the only organisms that would survive.

2

Once I am awake, for better or ill, I know that further attempts at sleep would be futile. I stretch arms and legs wide, arching my spine and reaching out like a seastar, letting my fingertips brush the smooth concave curve of the glass wall of the tank.

My movement alerts AIDA, the AI Deepwater Assistant, and this triggers the purge valve switch discreetly hidden in the wall joint. I listen to the quiet hum of the vacuum pumps whirring to life, the two tiny thumps as the connector tubes close to protect the other organisms that are dependent on the aquatic biome.

"It's a beautiful morning, Athes." AIDA greets me, her machine voice carefully coded to mimic the idiosyncrasies of human vocalization. Her message varies slightly every day, perhaps to approximate the variations in natural conversation.

"Weather? Water conditions?" I ask, never bothering to address it by name. I know that others do so, but it seems silly to me to pretend I am having a conversation when the other party is a machine. 'She,' AIDA, is a psychological comfort to some, but as for myself, I never want to forget that 'she' is a tool. A highly advanced, programmed companion, coworker, resource.

I listen absentmindedly as AIDA provides reports on surface conditions, water temperature, and seismic activity from the depth sensors in the trench below us.

As the water recedes, I remain suspended in it for the few moments it takes to reach transition depth, and then allow the altered biodynamics shift to pull my feet to the floor of the tank and assume an upright position. This transition from buoyancy to gravity always feels unnatural to me, even now, after more than twenty years of the routine. The weightlessness and unencumbered freedom of the water are traded for this slow, burdened bipedal slog.

I smile. I do sometimes have the dramatic, illustrative mind of a poet, but it is tempered by the pragmatism of a scientist. I begrudgingly accept my need for gravitationally based activity to maintain muscle tone and preserve the ability to perform several critical physical functions. This was a lesson learned by humans in space exploration over two centuries ago; however, my neutral buoyancy could have the same adverse effect on my bipedal function if I spent my entire life in the tank.

Water vacations have demonstrated many of the same effects on my body that they did on those mythical astronauts. Muscle atrophy and bone loss have been measured whenever I experienced prolonged immersion. Now, unless there is a compelling reason otherwise, I spend at least part of each day doing land-based activity to avoid any weakening of my back and leg muscles. Amphibious I may be, but my corporeal structure is still essentially primatoid, and such a physiologic deficit would eventually have a detrimental effect on my aquatic locomotion because I still depend on my legs and spine.

Evolution is slow. I came across an old saying in one of the Terra novels in the ArKive, referring to something occurring at a 'glacial pace.' I think the world reached a place where that definition no longer applied. When the Earth was burning, the glaciers melted quickly enough.

But adaptive change, especially in primates, is epochal. What was accomplished in me is the equivalent of the first ineffectual stumble of a toddler. Not an actual step forward, but a life-changing event. The species needs that stumble to survive. But after my birth, the progress stalled, sputtered, ground to a standstill. We have been unable to reproduce the result.

I spend some time staring out at the open ocean on the other side of the glass barrier, contemplating another life, one where I am ignorant of the pressures of this one, where daily I am tied to the failures of my progenitors. Of myself. Too much depends on what we do here to ruminate for long. Creatures I view from the inside, looking out, seem at peace with an existence that has largely been unchanged for millennia.

A slight tightening of the skin near the corners of my eyes brings me back to the present.

"Mist tank to saturate." My request activates a water feature built into the sidewall of the tank, replenishing the essential moisture I require to survive. A blast of salinized droplets fills the now emptied chamber, the briefest sustaining rainshower. Warmer than the ambient temperature maintained in the tank, this maneuver invariably fogs the glass.

It is impractical to use the mist outside the tank, as the rest of the lab is a dry habitat, so I stand at the door of the pressurization chamber between tank and lab.

AIDA's sensors respond to my proximity to the doorway. Security protocols trigger the biometric scanner, and I wait, less than patiently. The three seconds it takes AIDA to analyze the telemetry and biomorphology is barely more than a pause. Still, I wonder how much time I have wasted in the Aquadomes waiting for ingress and egress.

The feature is more important for the engineering ports, where technicians and scientists enter and leave the open ocean. Not allowing every sea creature to trigger the doors and gain entry is essential. Those divers don't want a shark following them into the moon pool. I live alone, but of course no one will hear of selectively disabling the protocol for personal convenience. We don't live in that world anymore. Not that I ever did.

So, I wait for confirmation, which is simply AIDA's crisp, clinical declaration.

"Bioorganism detected. Species indeterminate.
Category: Humanoid. Confirmed resident of habitat."

Once this proclamation is complete, the door opens, and I step through, taking a minute to zip myself into my 'drysuit.' In wet conditions, clothing is not really a necessity for me. But moisture is inconvenient and impractical around sensitive calibrated laboratory equipment and electronics. I must wear this unique garment that does the reverse of what a wetsuit does for humans when they must spend a prolonged amount of time in the water; it keeps my amphibious epithelium moist and prevents critical moisture loss while I am outside the tank. It is modified for my particular requirements but otherwise looks exactly like the 'coresuit' all the other scientists wear.

Like in space, the sea is cold, and our systems work hard to maintain warmth. To balance our use of resources and practice some responsible efficiency, our clothing is designed to provide insulation as well as cover, and our suits – mine included – collect and internally reflect our body heat.

The one I wear has an aqueous layer that circulates water between my skin and the suit. It is somewhat oxymoronic to call it a drysuit given its purpose, but wetsuit was already taken, in use for centuries before I needed such a thing. The suits are the love child of a collaboration between NASA engineers who modified the Xcel Infiniti wetsuit to satisfy their needs back in the Aquarius Reef days, and they have continuously improved them to address the evolving need.

Once in the suit, I wait at the entrance to the lab for AIDA to let me in.

"Laboratory access granted. Clearance level five."

I have no real idea what my clearance level means. Five sounds high if one assumes it would be impractical to have too many levels. I suspect no one has a level one. They are very attuned to psychological motivation, and I suspect they manipulate what we hear and perceive to reduce stress.

3

"Coffee is up." AIDA's voice surrounds me as I leave the airlock and head for my desk.

"Thank you," I reply. The mug on my side of the vacuum door is filled with a hot brew that approximates what coffee used to be. But this beverage contains a cocktail of essential amino acids and vitamins that we all require and would otherwise struggle to get from our limited diet in this brave new world.

When I see the mug, I smile at this repeated attempt at humor. AIDA has been programmed to learn about human diversion. It is not the nuanced exercise that comes naturally to people, but something that approaches it. AIDA has been instructed to provide my beverages in this particular cup occasionally. Again, healthy psychological distractions are necessary for maintaining mental resilience. I'm sure they have that written down in a manual somewhere.

The mug is a relic from the old Aquarius Reef I, its green logo from a chain coffee shop that could be found on every corner in Terra. The mermaid is a tongue-in-cheek reference to an imaginary construct of an amphibious humanoid, but her flowing hair and scaly duplicated tail are no reflection of what science constructed in me.

My interface is of a decidedly neutral color, favoring no single race, but invoking all of them, a grayish tan color with chromoclastic spots whose specialized pigments would assist me in absorbing sunlight energy. My skin is referred to as an 'interface' to acknowledge its critical function in oxygen exchange, particularly in an aquatic setting. It is probably also a way to deflect certain unpleasant aspects of my appearance and separate me from my human counterparts. Some humans still need to distance themselves from what is different to function societally.

I am alopecic, without apparent gender–identifying external organs, and there are pronounced but not excessive webs between the digits of my hands and feet. These are too elastic and unrestrictive to be termed syndactylic, as they do not negatively impact the dexterity of my hands. Indeed, they improve the functionality of my feet. Alas, I have no flowing tresses, no fluke or sparkling tail.

I have always been told I am beautiful, but I recognize I am only ever seen through a lens. My own, which has only the mirror for company, as the other faces I look upon each day are simply reminders of my relative inhumanity. The scientist in me appreciates the bilateral symmetry, pleasing and not grotesque, the large, jewel–like eyes and shapely head are my most human features, preserved enough to be confirmative of human ancestry.

The other lenses vary, creations of the individual beholder, which may range from admiration of the exotic to a more hopeful lens that yearns for this form to be the cradle which carries our species into the future. I am rarely exposed to those who see me only through a lens of disgust – my biological mother, when my curiosity got the better of me. Or a lens of jealousy, like the wife of one of the senior engineers for our biocomplex, whose husband waxes eloquent about my *potential* when he has had too much to drink. What he suspects that potential may be is always in question and best left alone. I benefit from the barriers they have erected against me.

I was to be the herald of our next great evolutionary leap, the salvation of a human race forced to abandon life on the surface of the planet and seek refuge in the one place they hadn't tried to live. But only by virtue of hanging from the wrong branch of the evolutionary tree. In theory, we all came from the sea, when the world was still a cauldron of simmering possibility.

Though humans never lived in the water doesn't mean that they didn't try to wreck the oceans, but they got lucky. The oceans survived the insult of twelve billion people living on a planet ideally made for only half that burden. When the magnetic shift of the Earth's atmosphere led to rapid changes in weather and the possibility to survive on the surface was lost, *terra firma* was abandoned for *aqua fluida*.

To understand it, you must understand how Terra
ended.

4

The ArKive contains fairly unflinching accounts of most of the highlights of human history. It was created, I am told, as honestly as possible so that future generations could learn from the mistakes of their forebears. It houses and catalogs everything from cooking lessons to university curricula to music. Images of art and photography from Terra preserve cultural achievements.

It informs me that my mother was a bioengineer who had been an Olympic transoceanic swimmer. My father was the world's best free diver. She had become fascinated with the field of bioengineering and genetics during her tenure as a world-class competitor in endurance aquatics. She was the subject of a ground-breaking scientific paper when it was discovered that her genetic profile had been altered sometime during her development as a water endurance athlete.

It shouldn't have been surprising. DNA responds to several stimuli, stressors can alter it, but some of the changes can become permanent adaptations to a new environment. The phenomenon had been shown over a century prior in astronauts, specifically in twins, one of which had spent an inordinate amount of time in space, while his brother maintained earthbound duties. Because their DNA was identical, it was easy to chart and track alterations when they occurred in the sibling with significant zero-grav exposure. While the changes were almost entirely reversed when he returned to Earth, these findings led to further studies of the effects of ultra-human endeavors on DNA.

Open-water swimming wasn't accepted as an Olympic sport until the latter part of the twenty-first century. It was primarily felt to be too unwieldy to manage safely, especially in the open expanses necessary to do the swimming equivalent of an ultra-marathon. Weather changes could be swift and severe, and pelagic predators were always a concern. A few smart pioneers mapped out the best time of year and optimal GPS locations for the events. Eventually, smart devices that emitted noxious stimuli kept the sharks and most of the larger jellies at bay. The sport began to get serious attention as the ultimate test of human endurance.

My mother's VO2 max scores were unprecedented, and she exhibited none of the differences that had been previously observed in swimmers when compared to runners on the treadmill. Her numbers were like those of ultramarathoners, and her pull tests were still superior to runners consistent with past studies, those groundbreaking observations about performance that were made as early as the twentieth century. Because she was an elite athlete with every possible privilege, she had been studied extensively from the time her athletic career started in high school.

The changes observed in her DNA were expected, driven by stress, changes in immune response, and thermal loss from prolonged immersion and elemental exposure. But she was a curious soul, listening and tracking her science as it evolved. When an injury finally curtailed her last chance at another qualifying swim, she used her convalescence to help work the data, and she was hooked.

She pursued degrees in medicine and biophysiology. Her Ph.D. paper bordered on science fiction, edging far closer to fiction than science, but her theories and her reasoning were sound, and humanity's need was great. Indeed desperate. Human aquatic physiology studies had advanced significantly, and she was rewarded with significant funding.

Although space had once been considered the off-Earth escape plan once the planet died, we, as a species, ran out of time to make the necessary advances needed to make that a viable frontier for survival. We had to find another alternative.

At the time, both NASA and NOAA were operating underwater laboratories that became temporary ocean habitats for the scientists and technicians who lived and worked in them. The Aquarius Reef Project had straightforward applications to the space-race due to the microgravitational properties of buoyancy. Now that the species was faced with extinction-level environmental pressure due to climate change, humans needed a survival plan that could be deployed with some haste.

The planet was still mostly water, and that fact became increasingly more apparent, as sea levels encroached upon and reclaimed all the formerly coveted vacation sites.

The San Andreas Catastrophe was the wake-up call. Twenty-five million souls were lost when the fault suffered a disastrous and fatal collapse, most of them to the sea, but plenty of people were crushed in the aftershocks, which registered above nine on the Richter magnitude scale. Five million more lives were lost in the unrelenting gas and brush fires. Enough ash covered the globe to create an atmospheric winter, and there were inadequate food stores and health supplies to address the needs of the surviving refugees.

Many people desperately scrambled eastward, even as far north as the Puget Sound, where Pacific flooding due to non-adaptive water rise claimed even more people. They didn't prepare, but how could they? Another example of human arrogance. They thought they were safe in the subduction zone.

Safe? The harbor lighthouse in Ashtabula, Ohio, was designated the easternmost casualty of the Catastrophe. The third grade Social Studies textbook in the ArKive documents that the city received government funds set aside for San Andreas relief.

The Aquarius Reef Project, which had at one time been threatened with closure due to lack of funding, was quietly being expanded as our most viable 'off-Earth' survival alternative. Belated attention was turned to addressing ocean pollution and dying coral with varying degrees of success. The Aquarius Reef Project was renamed Aquaria, in an attempt to soften what sounded like an experiment into something that seemed more like an exclusive resort, with individual divisions, or Aquadomes, that would house the population of this new underwater existence.

I have studied with wonder and sadness the predictive charting that was created by top scientific teams, most of whom must have understood that they would never survive to enjoy the fruits of their smart and frantic labors. They applied themselves to this problem of human survival with intelligence and hale-fellow-well-met optimism that I suspect was the result of the false promises of government leaders that those involved in the planning could somehow secure a place in the Aquadomes for their own children.

Earth was increasingly referred to as Terra; I think to lessen the crippling nostalgia for a home that would no longer exist as a viable option for us. Or perhaps (and more likely) it was to whitewash our sins of pollution and planetary climate destruction by referring to our planet in the obscurity of a romanticized concept.

But human survival was only going to be secured with the most draconian of maneuvers. The most optimistic projections suggested that only a fraction of a percent of the population could survive. The public was told next to nothing, and patronizing propaganda was put forth, indicating that a random lottery would determine which families would be relocated to undersea habitats. People were led to believe that fairness would be a consideration, but how could it be? It was a ploy to prevent anarchy, to foment an elusive order. Any blot on the record would disqualify a person from consideration for relocation.

There were apparently a privileged few who believed that their money would sway any adverse decision in their favor. For the first time in civilized history, money could not buy happiness. The principle of eminent domain was more applicable to world events than ever, and private funds were shamelessly siphoned to build a better world. Literally, the entitled rich were no more. The luxury of classism had to be abandoned for survival.

In the end, worldwide, less than one hundred thousand human beings are living and working in the Aquadomes. Each community represents its parent continent from Terra, both in population and prevailing cultural norms. Our North American Aquadome houses around forty-five hundred people.

These Aquanauts became the new colonizers of a watery frontier. One they hoped would sustain them, as the Earth they left behind became a mass grave of near extinction.

The criteria for inclusion were clear. The advantage was to the engineers, builders, divers, and scientists who could construct and maintain such a habitat, and had the vocational strengths needed to sustain it. To those with a secret list of preferred traits to ensure both genetic diversity and mental resilience.

Like my parents.

I use the term 'parents' very loosely. Imagine that I place the word in quotations, perhaps nontraditionally, and not without a bit of cynicism and irony if I am to disclose my position honestly.

My mother, the scientist, was being paid to engineer *adaptive humans*. That was the euphemism for human embryo manipulation justified by the impending relocation to Aquaria. Her methods would never have made it past an institutional review board on Terra. Her ultimate directive was to create a survivor race of merpersons.

I've even read a great deal on the promising background work, based on DVIG selective protein identification perfected nearly two hundred years ago by a pioneering Japanese geneticist named Himura. She contributed what was perhaps humanity's greatest genome-level interventional strategies beginning in the late twentieth century, and vestiges of her corporation, Rising Sun Industries, survive in the labs of Aquaria, in the Asian Aquadome. Dr. Himura's sequenced genome ark includes many prehistoric creatures and can be accessed from the ArKive.

My mother used her ova for this wholly *in-vitro* development. Because I survived embryonic chaos, that technicality makes her my mother.

My father, the free diver, was a man she had never even met, never exchanged a word with, probably never even considered in his entirety as an organism, so engrossed was she with the potential of one of his bodily fluids. He was one of many tapped as optimal sperm donors.

While it sounds romantic, swimmer-girl-meets-diver-boy, they fall in love and baby makes three, just consider my existence the redux version. Egg, sperm, scramble, thousands of embryos that — excuse me, who - didn't tolerate the insult of an attempt to insert gill development into their DNA.

Still, one, myself, survived swim bladder introduction and formed an adaptive amphibious interface. Should I mention that my most useful mutations came from neither of the humans, instead from an incredibly unique frog that spent its entire life underwater? So, not romance. Porn. Human-human-frog *ménage-a-troix*. And a sprinkling of saltwater fish DNA just for good measure.

Telmatobius culeus is an aquatic frog that lived in an oxygen-rich freshwater environment, at altitude, no less. Like myself, it had lungs and was theorized to have the amphibious ability to breathe air. It had adapted to perform critical oxygen exchange through its redundant skin, which had evolved multiple folds to increase surface area. The frog would do 'push-ups' when needed to increase water flow around the skin and facilitate oxygen uptake. Its DNA gives me my extra-human capabilities. I accessed a picture of one through the ArKive. As Terra neared its demise, National Geographic created a Photo Ark to preserve something of the animal species that inhabited it. The little guy looks like an amphibious older man in very baggy Terran clothing. I'm understandably nostalgic about it.

The result of my birth and subsequent survival is exceptionally romantic. Humans have a chance. Understanding me, the organism, may provide a bridge to a species equipped for life in the ocean.

Or incredibly tragic if I, the scientist, cannot find the means to reproduce myself. A conundrum of Shakespearian proportions, certainly.

I retrieve the mug, and I sigh as the hot liquid redistributes its warmth to my core.

"Play Schubert's *Trio in E Flat, Opus 11*," I request, and the gentle, ponderous piano introduction fills the lab, a calm background with which to start the day.

"Entry request logged. Subject: Dr. Rantha." AIDA alerts me a moment later.

"Accept request," I reply, crossing to the accessory tank across from the workbench. "Good morning, Triton." I greet the stalwart Japanese moor that is my biocompanion. To stave off loneliness, those who have no family have a pet fish. Mine is a decorative carp, a *koi*, with gauzy black fins and the exophthalmia that marks his species.

AIDA's response is predictable. "Bioorganism detected. Species: Homo sapiens. Confirmed resident of habitat. Laboratory access granted. Clearance level four."

"How did you sleep?" Thida, my research colleague, enters with her own mug in hand. She is making small talk in place of a greeting, although it is not merely the polite morning banter of a friend. I am, despite my usefulness to the science team as a researcher, still and always a specimen.

"Very well, thank you," is my automatic reply. I have never shared anything about the dreams with anyone. I do have private thoughts and observations that I can keep to myself as well, but there is little else.

I am catalogued in every way possible, and although I have never been studied in what should be my extended habitat, the ocean, all other forms of data possible are recorded. What and when I eat. How much I sleep and how often. Waste volumes, body heat, caloric spend, oxygen exchange. My apartment is well-appointed, but it is adjacent to my laboratory space and connected to the tank.

"Hello, Triton."   Thida greets him, too. She puts her face near the tank and watches him hovering. "He looks well," she tells me, taking a sip of her coffee.

Triton is more than a pet. He has been genetically modified for a saltwater environment. His tank biome is connected to mine. Stasis is maintained by computer, and on occasion, when my tank is full, he has visited me there, happily exploring, seemingly jealous of my space. But this is rare, as he is only fed at his end of the habitat, and Triton is not one to miss a meal. I know they watch him to evaluate the health of our biome. He is a bit like a canary in a coal mine. If he suffers ill effects, adjustments must be made so that I will not be similarly exposed or affected.

"He visited you while you slept last night," Thida
teased, knowing that I have not yet had an opportunity
to run through the data cache from the night before.

"One of these nights, he is going to surprise you and
turn into a dragon," I tell her, hiding my expression
behind the mermaid mug.

"If that happens, you will finally get your wish," she
replied, putting herself directly into my view for the first
time. She sets her coffee on the benchtop before sinking
onto the stool next to it. She wears a long-sleeved
cotton t-shirt over her coresuit, a direct violation that
we both know is unlikely to be logged or commented
upon, and her hair on this morning was a striking shade
of electric orange. I didn't miss it when she came into
the lab; she is positioning herself to be noticed.

"Yes, everyone will be more interested in him than they
are in me," I grumble, but good-naturedly. Thida has
never treated me like a specimen, but I have no way of
knowing if it is because she has been given a
psychosocial directive, or if it is a genuine feature of her
character. Just like I notice that her security level is
different than mine, but I refuse to ask what it means. I
suspect she knows the answer.

We did our university studies together some years ago. I
would guess Thida to be about thirty-six years old now,
so she has lived in the habitat since she was eight years
old. She and her mother were among the last persons

rescued from Terra; her father is the chief geneticist of
the Asian Aquadome community. She knows him only
through email and old photos; when it was time to stage
their departure from Aquarius Reef 1, he was still in
Malaysia. His unspoken influence on her career choice
is poignantly clear.

"Orange?!" I appraise her hair with interest, probably
because I have none of my own. Also, because this is a
subject I can get her warmed up to. She will go off on
this tangent gladly, and I can feel more like a regular
person having a conversation with a colleague for a few
precious minutes more before we inevitably return to
the subject of our work.

Thida was enamored of any chemical offshoots of our
education solely for her own selfish ends. Scientists are
problem-solvers, and that trait often is borne out in a
secondary creative drive that can be surprisingly well-
developed, such as virtuoso musical talent or hobbyist
painting. Color is Thida's drug, and colors are muted
and blunted to our eye in an underwater environment.
She admitted to me once that she recalled little of her
life on Terra other than the vividness of its colors.
Many chemical reactions are colorful, particularly those
with azo-compound byproducts.

She realized that if she slept with a UV mask on her
hair, she could induce premature whiteness. Her hair
became the palette upon which she displayed her artistic
expression. That and do-it-yourself haircuts make for

some interesting reveals. Some women have a beauty that cannot be marred by a lousy haircut, no matter how extreme. Thida is stunning, and she knows it.

"You don't like it?" Thida's smile is mischievous. She could care less about what I think. It is apparent that she is incredibly pleased with it.

"Contrary," I say with nonchalance, not wanting to make it too easy for her. "It's only my new favorite." I avoid making direct eye contact with her, turning instead to type my entry signature into the console. The screen holograph hovers before me at eye level, and I pretend to start looking at my messages.

Her scream of delighted laughter creates a sonic disturbance that subtly thuds against the glass between the two labs. Hers is opposite mine, with her domicile behind. It transmits a soft boom, like a heartbeat, from her space to mine. Close as we are, we don't even breathe one another's air.

For the next seven minutes, she regales me with her process of perfecting the color profile. Finally, when she can see me slumping visibly on my stool, she relents. Then teases, "There's more to it. But I will show you that *after* work."

8

We turn our attention to the data cache, quickly reviewing biodata collected overnight, and examining the graphs as though this has the potential to hold any fascination whatsoever for us. It does not, cannot, any longer. After years of graphing my biostatistics, we are numbed to the overwhelming evidence of ongoing homeostasis.

In fact, the data is so dull that we both know any deviation will stand out like a beacon, when, or if, it ever occurs. I am a healthy – or at least unchanging - whatever-I-am. In theory, reproduction should be feasible.

In practice, it presents obvious problems. There is no other organism with which to accomplish such a feat. Although my human DNA suggests that I am genetically female, my appearance is more gender-fluid, more in keeping with my amphibious relations.

"AIDA, bring up tissue culture specimens from Plate series 21J and embryos from series 71CA5405 through 5445 and 74ZQ5812 through 5927." Thida is all business now, for which I am grateful. Our project requires precision and focus.

"Rantha, Dr. Thida Ananya, voice signature confirmed. Require Athes 47AA1218 to release."

"Athes confirming request," I reply.

"Series 47AA1218, Athes, voice signature confirmed. Specimen and embryo delivery complete."

Several years ago, I consented to laparoscopic biopsy of pelvic structures hypothesized to be gonadal. Additionally, tissue was harvested from both my vestigial lung structures as well as the swim bladder wall along my spine. These interventions were elucidative in two ways.

First, the gonadal tissue did harbor harvestable pluripotent cells that we continue to believe are reproductive. Second, the swim bladder organ was significantly more caudal and more ventral than expected, and it is not a feature of aquatic frogs. There was no additional DNA found in my profile other than *Homo sapiens* and *Telmatobius*, so it was initially unclear why the swim bladder had developed.

Genome sequencing appeared to suggest a contaminant that was close to that of some species of Antimora, a saltwater fish with relatively primitive origins. This finding led one of the lead scientists in my mother's lab to suggest the genesis of my survival as an organism required activation of dormant DNA. It was an astonishing and secondary discovery of profound proportions.

But it should not have been. It has long been accepted that some poor prehistoric bastard was the first to step out of the primordial ooze and onto dry land, and from that hapless creature, even more elaborate carbon-based life-forms evolved. The potential for the return of water adaptations has been there all along in our DNA, dormant in the face of evolutionary stimuli that were probably not coming.

And those evolutionary pressures were not necessarily present in any profound way during my embryonic development. It was unclear to me how it had been accomplished, and what I would come to discover would be my undoing.

Those preliminary findings solved one of the issues. Pluripotential cells could be a vehicle for cloning. It gave us hope that there was an in vitro solution to the problem of advancing the species as a race of aquatic hybrids. My gonadal cells could be enucleated, and the genetic material from one of my fully developed mature cells introduced. These cells could be cultured, and if any viable embryos resulted, all our hard work and sacrifice would be rewarded.

We turned to the biohood to examine the specimens that AIDA had retrieved.

"Cellular aggregation failure in two, five, six, eight through ten, fourteen, seventeen, and twenty. Cellular degeneration and death in one, four, twelve, thirteen, and eighteen. Failed substrate attachment in three, seven, and nineteen. Bacterial overgrowth and contamination in eleven, fifteen, and sixteen. Terminate culture series. Prepare new plates." I dictated in a tone far more dispassionate than I felt.

"Termination request initiated." AIDA's voice flooded the lab.

"Secondary request confirmation granted," Thida spoke by rote, her tone no less neutral. Only her expression revealed what she felt. Another month's maneuvering, another failure to achieve growth thresholds.

"Termination request logged. Commencing termination sequence Plate series 21J. Plate series 21K preparation queued pending sample harvest."

"I think you'd better not save the surprise for later," I told Thida, and was surprised when I felt her hand rest gently on my upper thigh. I glanced down at it and back up at her. I could see the tears forming and knew she would loathe herself if they fell, but I couldn't look away.

9

The history of mammalian cloning was fraught with controversy and difficulty. The arguments began in the late twentieth century and never stopped. The more complex the organism, the more challenging to obtain a viable embryo. Successful clones were rare, and even when they survived, they seemed to have significantly curtailed lifespans, frequently related to congenital disabilities or deficit.

Over time, techniques were perfected that allowed certain smaller organisms, such as rodent clones, to achieve lifespans that approximated reported norms. But these lifespans were short to begin with, only one or two years in length. There was no consensus about whether such an accomplishment was any type of victory at all.

And because one of the strongest arguments against cloning was rooted in human morality and ethics, even the most successful labs were subject to direct scrutiny and skepticism designed to unmask the cheerful façade of these types of findings.

To achieve an expected lifespan in a cohort of twenty rodent clones required the harvest (and none too occasional death of the donor) of close to thirty thousand ova in a project that spanned just under four decades of work. Achieving a laudable result came at a cost greater than the gain.

But in our case, I only had a finite number of harvested cells. Swabs from my oral cavity were implanted without success. We appeared to get some initial positive development using cell scrapings I gathered from my epithelium, but for some reason, these harvest sites were taking a long time to heal. We had to reharvest repeatedly because my tissues would not grow in standard culture media.

Another time, a more severe skin infection resulted in a secondary swim bladder infection, a setback that resulted in the need for broad-spectrum antibiotics and aspiration of the organ. I was in pain and unable to maintain buoyancy, unable to sleep in my tank.

Reciprocal sickbay pods are a part of our laboratory layout, and I languished in one with Thida nursing me back to health, using access ports and barrier gloves to reach through and provide my care. Saline mists kept my interface moist, and the greenhouse effect within my enclosed pod helped regulate my temperature.

I remember when I began to feel well again because suddenly, I was hyperaware of Thida's touch. Even though the system was a decontamination/negative pressure setup, and despite the thick glove ports we used, I could read something in the way she cared for me. It bothered me.

I was indeed a sacrifice to science, but Thida didn't seem to have a life to speak of outside our laboratory universe. Her only visitor was her mother, who was kind enough to bring enough home cooking for both of us when she needed to visit us in the sunlight zone.

When Thida's touching became more personal, I assumed she must be lonely in all the ways any organism can be. All my suspicions about her placement could have been confirmed with a question, but I would never put her in a position to have to answer it. If our betters had asked her to make a sacrifice for science, give up any claim to a family of her own for the distinction of working with a novel species, I didn't want to know about it. Nor did I want someone that I would potentially spend the rest of my life with to have to visibly squirm in acknowledgement or just as boldly lie about what we both knew was the truth. Neither would I fault her for it. Had our places been exchanged, the appeal would be just as evident to me, the scientist. You don't pass on such a unique opportunity. It's bigger than you are. For a young scientist, it would be a career-maker.

When we had been paired in the pod a decade earlier, I had suspected that such an arrangement had been to give me a consistent research companion. It may have also provided our superiors with an observer who would commit to the long haul of untangling the Gordian knot of my existence.

The long years of shared experience and responsibility would bond us and make it difficult for Thida to abandon the project. It also made her more malleable ethically. It made whatever interventions were needed normal and necessary, and we both had to buy into the project together, which looks strangely like I am giving consent from her perspective. It would assuage a great deal of conflict or latent guilt, the illusion that I have a choice in all of this.

But I understood loneliness, both as a construct and as a reality of my unique existence. There was no other of 'my kind' from which to create a community. I belonged to the humans; their hopes hung on our success.

After so much time had passed, I initially assumed that she was reacting to a fear that she could lose me. I thought it sympathy for the dying; I already suspected that if I ever really got into any serious health trouble, their interventions would be well-intentioned guesswork that could just as quickly kill me as cure me.

But when I turned the corner and was on the mend, the quality of her touch did not change. It was no longer clinical, that artificial gentleness born of training; it was care, it was empathy, it was intimacy.

I couldn't afford to respond to it. I cannot contribute to such blatant manipulation, either of myself or Thida. Which is the worse, I don't pretend to know.

Thankfully, now, Thida quickly recovers, her smile sputtering only a moment after our grim discoveries before recovering its usual wattage.

"AIDA, go to UV-A spectrum in the lab for twenty seconds." Thida cannot suppress her pleasure at the prospect of her surprise.

"UV-A exposure-" AIDA attempts to give us the standard warnings, but Thida is having none of it. "AIDA, override warning message, and execute." Thida interrupts. AIDA can be infuriating, but if you override too many warnings, the system reports your entire log for evaluation, exposing your every utterance to the record. Thida does not appear to be concerned about this. I am. If they heard every off-color observance I have made, they would probably jettison me out to sea. Then again, maybe not.

"UV-A spectrum, laboratory lighting, duration twenty seconds, commencing."

And when the lights switch over, I see what all the secretiveness and dramatic buildup was preparing me to see: Thida's new hair color fluoresces under the black light, glowing bright blue. It is pretty awesome.

"Now I can compete with you," she laughed, admiring my chromoclasts, which were lit up like stars, illuminating a pattern on my skin that was otherwise subtle and difficult to see with the naked eye.

I could sense she was studying me intently, so I whispered, "Worth the wait."

She was quiet and said nothing other than "Resume laboratory-standard illumination." This command brought the fluorescent spots back on, and although she turned back to the hood to commence the examination of the embryos, and I was unable to see her face, I could tell she was pleased with my response.

10

I had finally become inured to non-viable embryos. It took longer for me to get there than Thida, but I suppose it makes some kind of twisted sense. All scientists must find a way to build up defenses against despair when the inevitable work failures occur. She had a shorter path to feigned disinterest; after all, these organisms *are* my relatives.

The process itself is mind-numbing because you must read every number out loud so that AIDA can document the results. Every number in the series, followed by that word, like a small blow every time. Non-viable.

But this time, I pause. 74ZQ5837 remains viable. Thida looks up from her notes in response to the silence.

"I guess your glowing hair brought us luck," I tell her, and see that she doesn't yet make the connection. I connect the dots for her, and this time, no amount of clinical remove can hide the smile in my voice.

"Embryo 74ZQ5837. Viable. Sequester for passthrough protocol and focus. Initiate continuous telemetry."

"Commencing continuous telemetry on 74ZQ5837. Isolation initiated, sequester and sequence record created. Calculating implantation timeline." AIDA confirms.

"Unmute telemetry audio file. Play continuous," I instruct.

"Won't that drive you crazy?" Thida asks, marveling that we will be listening to the tiny heartbeat in real-time.

"Less crazy than not knowing whether it is still with us," I tell her. "Besides, you won't hear it when you go back across to your side of the hab."

"Good point," she agrees, but I barely hear her, having returned to the remaining burden of the 74ZQ embryos, the rest of which have not survived.

We continue our daily routine tasks to the staccato pulse that is our new friend 74ZQ5837. This soundtrack is ultimately soothing and bothers Thida less than she assumed it would. I can see she is not-so-secretly triumphant. I cannot quite match her enthusiasm, and I frown at her suggestion that the embryo needs a name. Perhaps I am too – what? Cynical? Superstitious?

"Come on, why not? It survived. Would you want to be called 74ZQ5837?" Thida asks, arching her eyebrows and then stops herself.

"Like 47AA1218?" I asked her, repeating my own series number, which is still used to preface the name they eventually gave me. Athes. A blend of Athena and Pisces. The wise fish. But they never let go of the number, which is still the only way to access my file in the ArKive.

"Embryo implantation calculation complete. Optimal implantation day 47AA1218, Athes - 21K.24; Rantha, Dr. Thida Ananya – 36B.24." AIDA's timing is sometimes comical, and her notation interrupts our awkward discussion.

The number is calendar shorthand. Twenty-one refers to my twenty-first year, K denotes month 11 (alpha order puts K eleventh), and twenty-four means the twenty-fourth day of that month.

The Aquadome has no universal calendar. Calendar dates are calculated on a personal basis, not universally, ever since the Descent from Terra. Any date is entered into your calendar based upon where it falls in the year after your birthday. Thida's date differs from mine as she will only be in the second month following her birthday on the implantation date, and I will be in the eleventh month following mine. The days are numbered consistently within the month itself. The year is irrelevant.

I guess it is too tragic to contemplate any more extensive history other than that of the Dome. Those who are older can still calculate the Year based upon how much of their life has been spent underwater. Some still do, I suppose.

We took a break to eat our usual rations, and Thida supplemented it with a thick soup that her mother had prepared. It was her way of apologizing for our earlier awkwardness.

I put a saline tablet under my tongue in response to her nagging as she assessed my latest biochemical profile.

"Hey, let's check the healing on that harvest site," she reminded me. "We have to make sure it's pristine, or it will interfere with our implantation window."

Oh, right. I was about to become the surrogate for my clone. Obediently, I shrugged out of my drysuit and climbed into the examination pod, settling on the table face up. Thida closed the aperture, sealing the space, and pushed her hands through the glove box and adjusted the light source.

"Mist," I commanded, and AIDA sprayed me, moistening my skin and making me immediately more comfortable under the light.

"Alright, here we go," Thida gave her standard warning, so I closed my eyes and tried to distract myself from her touch.

She spent the next several minutes probing the edges of the harvest site, until she was satisfied with its positive progress. Just when I thought she was about to turn out the light and say goodnight and take her leave of me, she spoke. What she said was murmured so softly that I almost didn't catch it, but that was her point. She didn't want her statement to be sensed by AIDA or the recorders in the lab, and the hum of the examination pod masked it even more effectively.

"I'm going to try something new later. Don't be alarmed," Thida reassured me, but of course, such a statement only created personal turmoil. Curiosity to kill the cat.

"AIDA, let me out," she requested, waiting to be allowed to return to her quarters without a backward glance or another word.

11

I merely climbed out of the pod and made my shutdown circuit. I didn't bother to put my drysuit back on, only fed it into the UV sanitizer so it would be ready the next day. I flexed my liberated toes and padded across the lab to feed Triton, who made his usual kissing noises of gratitude at the surface of the tiny moon pool adjacent to the tank aerator.

"Lab systems, Nocturne level function. Criteria exceptions, life support, and designated critical function operations, maintain audio surveillance of 74ZQ5837." The command alerted AIDA to begin nighttime shutdown protocol.

Then I reversed my trip through the decomp chamber and stretched again before instructing AIDA to refill my tank. I concentrated then, satisfied that I could still hear the determined heartbeat of 74ZQ5837 before the rush of the tank pump obscured it. I let myself float upward with the water level, allowing my mind to drift. I reminded myself that if I was unable to sleep, I had a reading list queued up on the ArKive. Something to look forward to. Plan B. Or perhaps Plan A if I couldn't even *get* to sleep.

The pump was cycling down, the tank virtually full, when the power surged, faltered, and resumed almost immediately.   That got my attention because it seldom happened absent a storm or a seaquake, and neither had been forecast on the server alerts for the day. I swam to the glass wall that separated the tank from the lab and couldn't see anything alarming.

Then I thought of the embryo and had a moment of icy fear until I remembered that the generator backed up the life support. But it didn't appear to be a power failure, and the genny's indicator lights were not on. Everything was running off the grid.

I concentrated, less trying to listen than feel the sound transmitted through the water density and was relieved when I realized that I could hear 74ZQ5837 still plugging along. Maybe Thida had a point. Max or Zoe would have been less of a mouthful.

I listened some more and heard all the secondary sounds I was supposed to be attending, so I prepared to close my eyes. No sooner had I done so than I heard the decomp chamber flood ahead of the tank door opening. I turned in alarm, concerned that I had somehow triggered a wet decompression, but her shock of flaming hair easily identified the dark figure that came through the opening. Thida, in her wetsuit, wearing a GillMax tankless rebreather mouthpiece.

I worried that something was wrong, something had happened, but her fingers closed around my ankle, and she gave a playful tug before swimming away to the corner of the tank. I shook my head and blew bubbles in her direction, wondering what our lab director would make of this.

I followed her, and her eyes were dancing happily behind her mask. She took my hands and pulled me through the water, trying to get me to play along. It took me a few moments to understand that she was curious, and I had forgotten that she did not know what I was capable of in an aquatic environment.

I took hold of her forearms and gracefully pulled her behind me, maneuvering in graceful loops, effortlessly towing her with me through the water. Using my powerful feet to propel us, looping from corner to corner in a water ballet, trying to let her feel the freedom water gave me, how much it was like flying, pushing her and pulling her around me as though she weighed nothing. Well, next to nothing. Thida is compact, but humans are still moderately cumbersome in the water compared to me.

After a quarter of an hour, I towed her to the oceanside corner opposite the decomp chamber door, where there was a spout pool, with shallow steps up to a ledge for reclining out of the water. I deferred to her, urging her to climb up, while I sat on the step below her.

She was laughing before she could even free the Gill from her lips.

It was then that I realized that the surge had been her doing.

I waited for her to get settled and said, "Spill it."

She scrutinized my face for signs of censure and seemed relieved not to find any. "What can I say? I wanted to swim with you."

"You could have asked," I pointed out logically.

She shook her head vigorously, making her hair stick up. Even soaking wet, her appeal was undiminished. "I don't need AIDA to catalog everything."

I couldn't keep from laughing. "And how, exactly, are you planning to explain this?"

"We won't have to," Thida confided, and her tone suggested a guarantee. "I found a way to bypass our keeper."

I was still shaking my head, but I was certainly curious. Bypassing the system was an act of rebellion, and even absent surveillance, I was sure the system was sampling my water supply, and what were we to do when it discovered foreign DNA. DNA that could be traced to the ArKive catalog under Rantha, Dr. Thida Ananya. I waited patiently for her to explain it. Thida can be surprisingly stingy with details, especially when she has a story to tell. Better to let her tell it at her own pace.

"I've been reading about the history of AIDA's programming in the ArKive," she told me. "I always wondered how she…crap, *it*…knew what to respond to and what to ignore. Haven't you noticed that the system is creepy good at that?"

I had noticed but had not been sufficiently curious to read up on all those dry coding manuals in the ArKive. Now *there* was a cure for insomnia if ever I heard of one.

"It is surprisingly simple, really. The coders made a list of every idiosyncratic thing they could come up with and built it around a learning algorithm based on an IGNORE command." Thida could probably see my eyes glazing over, so she rushed to say, "Athes, keep up. Ignore. Get it?"

I didn't, but I nodded to encourage her to get to the point. "It is easier than teaching the program what not to do. Just ignore, ignore, ignore. But they never locked the command administratively. It's a loophole. Meaning a user can *actively* employ the IGNORE command to generate a window of privacy for whatever interval is desired.

"I tried it with something harmless, and then checked the log when the entries for the previous day were cached. The period in question didn't show up on the log."

A great log checker is Thida. It holds no interest whatsoever for me. I know I am required to open the cache and review it, but it is a cursory exercise, another box to check, not a thing of minutely fascinating details, as it is to my habitat-mate.

"But why the mini-surge?" I asked, now sure that Thida had caused the blip.

"Not sure," Thida admitted. "But I think AIDA has to mark the beginning time of the command, and power down until the interval is over."

"And how much time did you give yourself to commit this crime?" I asked, certain it would somehow backfire.

"About…" she looked charmingly confused and reached for my arm. I wore my watch faithfully; I wasn't even sure she knew where her own was at any given time. She twisted her head around to read the time. "Another seven minutes? And it isn't a crime…yet."

Apparently, she wasn't feeling the urgency of her time limit, as she slid languorously into the water next to me but didn't replace the Gill just yet. She rested her arms on my shoulders and didn't close her eyes to kiss me, observing me as her mouth explored to her satisfaction. She let go reluctantly and whispered close to my ear, "Maybe now it's a crime."

The kiss told me more than I wanted to know. I'm sure that what I gleaned from the encounter was not what Thida intended me to learn.

She secured the Gill between her teeth with a smile and disappeared below the water surface, popping back up a few moments later to murmur around the rebreather. "Totally worth it."

Then she was gone, with a last quick tug on my ankle, and I submerged in time to see her finning furiously toward the decomp chamber before she disappeared through the door. I heard the thump of the airlock several moments later when she made her escape through the lab.

12

My mind had plenty to process, but after a while, I stopped trying to analyze everything. I couldn't solve any of my dilemmas at that moment. I finally focused on the telemetry audio for 74ZQ5837 and listened, trying to exclude all other distractions. It became a remarkably effective meditative exercise, the lullaby by which I was able to find sleep.

But something woke me, and the quality of light in the lab made me confident that not much time had passed since I had drifted off. The soft illumination below the workbench was still at the nocturnal level. At a predetermined hour, adaptive brightness would gradually flood the workspace and our living spaces, increasing the lumens and simulating dawn, just as my orders the night before at shutdown did not immediately darken the laboratory. The light was gradually lowered, simulating dusk. It was the way circadian physiology was supported, and a diurnal rhythm was maintained.

I brought my wrist up in front of my face, adjusting my position to hover vertically in the tank. The movement triggered the illumination feature on the device, which confirmed my suspicion about the time. Less than two hours had elapsed since I had first closed my eyes.

I listened again, my brain discarding noises that were usually part of the biome until I could faintly discern one that didn't fit. I moved my head back and forth in the water, trying to pinpoint it, ultimately localizing it to an area in the bottom corner of the tank nearest the glass wall that separated the tank from the ocean.

I could hear movement in the subfloor that I had not noticed before, as if there were something of significant size on the other side of the metal platform that formed the floor. There was a square cap that could have been initially a hatch or a small access panel, but for the entirety of my time in the biome tank, it had been sealed.

Theoretically, I surmised, it might provide ingress from underneath, as an engineering failsafe of some sort. But it sounded as though water were flowing beneath it, and when I placed my feet on the floor of the tank, I could feel the transmitted thrum of a substantial force churning the seawater below me.

The floor sensors triggered a tank purge, and I waited for the water to finish draining before listening again. The sounds were only slightly more prominent and still too nonspecific to identify them and to make any sense of what might be causing them.

"Scan habitat, tank floor." My command echoed off the tank walls, and I thought, but couldn't be sure that there wasn't a whispery watery response from below.

"Tank floor, habitat, scan reveals one bioorganism. 47AA1218 Athes, species indeterminate. Category:

Humanoid. Confirmed resident of habitat." Okay. Using myself as a control gave AIDA a baseline, made me confident the system was functional and proved I was awake. Probably. Now, on to what I did not know.

"Scan habitat, subfloor level."

"Subfloor level, habitat, scan reveals one bioorganism. Species indeterminate. Category: Humanoid. Non-resident of habitat."

"Characterize structure location of non-resident bioorganism," I request, sounding far calmer than I feel. It must be a mistake.

"Structure specific inquiries require Engineering clearance. Cannot complete your request."

"Record and log telemetry scan of non-resident bioorganism," I respond.

"Non-resident bioorganism telemetry is not authorized. Dome regulation 1217-33-37.61b." AIDA counters unhelpfully.

"Confirm positive finding of foreign bioorganism, subfloor habitat." I am determined to gather as much information as I can; regulations be damned.

"Confirmed. Logged. Timestamp…" AIDA reads off the timing, and I register the numbers, but I have stopped listening to the remainder of the log update. I am trying to decide whether I can still hear the strange noises near the footplate.

"Repeat scan habitat, subfloor level in real-time."

"Repeat scan negative for life forms," AIDA reports.

I leave through the decompression chamber, and the lights come up marginally in the laboratory as I enter.

"Move telemetry for 74ZQ5837 to background. Notify of changes. Diurne illumination level, abort Nocturne protocol. Bring up ArKive, original blueprint for Science Level habitat domes." The hologram pops up at my station, and I scan it. AIDA may not be authorized to answer my engineering questions, but it cannot block my access to public records. "Magnify subfloor detail, ocean-facing, times two. Play Bach's *Partito number three in E-major, Gavotte en Rondeau,*" I add as an afterthought.

I spend some time zooming in and out on the blueprints, marveling at what I am seeing. There appears to be continuous water flow via redistribution channels through a circuit that connects to every pod on the Science Level. I check and recheck the dimensions of the circuit tubes, learning that their diameter is wide enough to allow an adult human to swim through them.

Or more specifically, SCUBA dive within them, since the channels are always flooded. The circuit is open to the ocean but does not communicate with any waste channels. It appears to be used for subfloor maintenance access to the habs. But even if an engineer were down there, why at night? And any of the maintenance crew would scan as identifiable residents of the habitat.

I go back and forth, viewing and reviewing the specs. In every separate living space, the footplate appears to be functioning. The one on the floor of my tank is welded closed, probably for integrity purposes related to my water biome. It could easily be accessed with a few minutes of torchwork if the tank above were empty. But there had been an unidentified humanoid inside the circuit. Not one of the habitat residents.

I stare through the glass divider into Thida's side of the lab, speculating that a functioning footplate must exist on the floor of her platform, in the living quarters behind the lab. Its position should be opposite the one on the bottom of the tank.

If I were correct, there was theoretically a way for non-lab personnel to access the main floor of the habitat. However, I suspected that AIDA had to unlock the hatches just as it would any other entrance.

Still, the more disturbing thought came swiftly on the heels of that one. There was only one place for an outside organism to access the circuit, only one place for an unidentified humanoid to get in. From the open ocean.

I would get no more sleep this night.

13

I logged my findings in detail and reported the event, following protocol to the letter.

I thought about waking Thida, but I didn't. I needed to decide how I was going to address what had happened between us. I needed to consider whether it might not be a coincidence that an unidentified humanoid had been in the water circuit beneath the hab just hours after Thida had breached my biome.

Then I decided I might as well get some reading done and confirmed that the log cache accurately listed the events of the prior evening, so whoever investigated it would have an accurate accounting of the details. I was satisfied with what I found, so I bookmarked the timestamp and amended my report with the tag.

Otherwise, the log revealed no other anomalies. Thida's stolen hour looked like any other period after lab shutdown. All quiet leading up to my encounter with the mystery guest.

I tried to concentrate on Greek mythology, but even that couldn't hold my attention.

I put an earpod into my left ear and used it to listen to a few isolated seconds of 74ZQ5837's telemetry. Still steady and robust. Then I turn my attention to the embryo's repeated sequencing, which triggers something I hadn't considered.

"Analyze water sample from water redistribution circuit traps for genetic material. Log results to 47AA1218 Athes." I want the answers, if any are forthcoming, to come to me first.

"Request received. Commencing analysis. Result compilation in approximately one hundred eighty-four minutes," AIDA replies. Since we routinely assess genetic material in our biome samples, I am hoping to get answers without drawing attention to my thought processes. At least not initially. The request will show up in the log cache after midnight tomorrow, but it gives me several hours to consider what I find before I can be questioned about it.

14

In twenty years, I have been out of my living quarters only a handful of times. Each time with supervision. We are all separated from one another, living in minidomes to decrease the amount of surface area exposed to the crushing pressure of the sea. Each minidome serves as laboratory and living space for its inhabitants. On the clearest days, when sunlight penetrates well, the other habitats built into the face of the reef look like large bubbles.

The dome system for North America is constructed just deep to the Key Largo shelf. The reef system is south by southeast of the Florida peninsula, still in the sunlight zone. Two score individual biodomes, each of which houses four scientists, are located at the shallowest depth, just 40 meters below the land shelf. The remaining domes are interconnected, slightly larger in size, and house family groups connected by radial spokes to a central gathering area. These are located an additional forty meters below the upper outpost.

The engineers who built the Aquadome system seem to appreciate our ocean home the most. Gone are many of the concerns about decompression, as all external dives are now essentially saturation dives, with the exception of surface equipment maintenance. The engineers and technicians live and work at similar depths. Way stations placed on the reef during construction are still used to refill SCUBA tanks, allowing for prolonged shift work outside the habitat. Crews can sustain exposures of up to twelve to fourteen hours.

The upkeep of the structural parts is brutal. Continuous surveillance of the integrity of the structure must be undertaken, with proactive planning to ensure pristine maintenance, prevent corrosion and water incursion events that could be catastrophic. The flooding or loss of one habitat could take out the communication and information grids for an entire continental system.

Weighted seismic sensors are deployed to the depths so that seaquake activity can be charted and followed. Weather balloons anchored to the reef are deployed to the surface to provide atmospheric information. There are larger, more permanent floating apparatuses, which also serve as communication links to the six other Aquadomes on the globe.

The domes were constructed and anchored into the underlying rock, with the reef running adjacent and downward. It is the most optimal protection from tropical storms. Aquarius Reef I had to be evacuated not infrequently due to hurricane effects on the coastal tidal areas. Humanity no longer has the luxury of abandonment, so the Aquaria Domes were placed to provide sustainable shelter in constantly and rapidly changing conditions.

It is commonplace to encounter engineers working on the ocean side of the tank glass, repairing, cleaning and maintaining visibility and function. For years, Jesús has been assigned to my habitat, and like clockwork, three times a week, two mornings and one evening, he is there, ready with a few gestures of encouragement. He, like Thida, provides the only continuity of human contact in my life.

When I first came to inhabit this place, I was still chronologically and physically a juvenile, although my academic development was accelerated over my chronological human peers. I was functioning at a college level when I was released from the Central Genetics laboratory and given my private biome. At around the same time, Thida moved in next door, and our formal university education began.

Jesús had probably been briefed about me, but then, I imagine everyone who was to come in contact had to be. Despite such a precaution, it was difficult for many of them to mask their reactions to seeing me for the first time.

Jesús did not appear to be overly surprised, disgusted, shocked, awed, or otherwise affected in any discernable manner, which was certainly a first. He simply waved at me through the glass, acknowledging me, as I assumed he would acknowledge any other human, but I already knew I was not human. He had to as well; it isn't as though I can hide my differences.

I waved back, and so curious about this anticlimactic development, pressed myself up against the glass, distorting my facial features. I'm not sure now why I did it, other than out of a distaste for any situation where I feel as though I might be on display. To my surprise, this made Jesús laugh, and in response, he pressed his lips against the inside surface of his full facemask and made a funny face. It was a seemingly genuine exchange, one creature to another, perhaps the evenest treatment I had ever received; he was treating me as an equal.

As time went by, he would pause for several minutes during each visit and make complicated gestures at me. I didn't understand them, but he made eye contact the entire time, so I knew he was making a sincere attempt at communication.

I consulted the ArKive to see if I could find a way to decipher his codes, initially wondering if it was some sort of military diver code. I knew there had always been amphibious units in the armed forces of many countries on Terra, most certainly they had methods for passing and receiving messages in the water. Many of the individuals that had helped build and establish the underwater colonies were former military personnel, with tech divers and engineers among them.

But I discovered that universal diver hand signals were far more rudimentary than what Jesus was using, and according to the ArKive, it was sign language. Jesús was deaf, and he had a ready way to communicate without talking. Perfect for fishbowl conversations, except this fish did not have that language. But my drive to make a connection with another being, any other being, was so strong that I programmed tutorials from the ArKive into my study schedule.

It took the best part of the next two years for me to master it. I did the alphabet first, so at least I could learn his name. I spelled out mine, and he responded in kind. I knew the mythology of the name, and he was amused at my reaction. I learned the signs for 'famous' and 'most important.' He was entertained. I looked forward to our visits and remained as determined as ever to assimilate his language.

It might have been simpler had there been any way for him to give me feedback. Or if I hadn't forced myself to turn away each day after wasting any more than five minutes of his time. I wanted to learn but did not want him to be in any trouble for talking to me. I was afraid if that happened, he would be reassigned elsewhere and never come back.

After a time, he understood what I was doing. He was patient, and little by little, I improved enough to have a conversation, encapsulated and understandable. Once I grasped it, he would tell me jokes. Or horrifying stories about the sharks around the reef, only letting me off the hook when my expression became too distressed. He was kidding, of course, but it was a great diversion.

Eventually, Jesús told me about his family and how he had come to Aquaria. He had helped design and build it. His hobby as a child on Terra had been spearfishing. He had to help feed his many siblings. I asked whether he had ever been afraid of the ocean, and he shook his head. He explained that on land, he was the outcast, silence surrounded him and isolated him. In the sea, the quiet of his existence was normal, forced upon any others that came with him underwater, but because he already knew it, he belonged.

He gestured at me. I nodded; I understood about being different.

But his hands were ever more insistent. I must understand about the sea, he observed, indicating my graceful turns in the water. His fingers made a circle around his facemask, letting me know how much he would love to be able to dive without any encumbrances, like me.

I shook my head. I had never been allowed out into the open water. I had no way to know whether I belonged there, or how such a thing would feel. The urgency of my signing signaled the urgency I felt in my heart. It conveyed a longing I had never admitted I felt.

Jesús didn't answer me for many days. He would wait outside the glass, telling me nothing and watching me swim for those few minutes each visit. When he finally brought his hands up again to communicate, his words were a poem of sadness and despair. He hadn't realized that he was the lucky one, free to know in his bones that the sea was his.

I was just a big fish in a bowl.

A wise fish, who knew I wasn't free.

15

This morning, I wished Thida knew sign language.

That way, we could privately process the events of the previous night. Not the former, which I wasn't ready to discuss, but the latter. I had to decide how I was going to tell her about it.

She came into the lab, and I should have worried because there was something in her eyes that I couldn't read. She greeted Triton, and pointedly touched my shoulder, leaning over me as if she were reading what was up on the holograph.

"The Director messaged me," she whispered, low enough that the fourth movement of the *Rondeau* gave her adequate cover. "She's on her way down to the habitat."

I hadn't received such a message, which seemed odd since the report of the night's events had originated with me. I couldn't decide whether I should or should not be surprised by this. And Thida's whispering had me wondering if she had been told not to warn me.

I tried to make light of it, though, whispering back, and acting purposefully obtuse, "Perhaps they think you are compromised."

Rather than answer, she frowned at me and moved away to the workbench. Her reaction confirmed my suspicion about the night before, and my instincts told me that it was something else I should be wary about.

"We should review the repeat sequencing on 74ZQ5837," she recommended in another voice as if all were business as usual. "I reviewed the log cache from last night," she added, knowing I would understand what she wasn't saying. Perhaps it was her way of signaling that my report was the reason for the unannounced visit.

"I still need to read the recommendations from the fertility specialists regarding hormone augmentation ahead of implantation," I replied, because I could think of no other diverting comment to make.

Just then, AIDA's voice interrupted as the external door to the suite opened. "Entry logged. Subject: Lipton, Director, Dr. Ari Elizabeth. Bioorganism detected. Species: Homo sapiens. Confirmed resident of habitat. Laboratory access granted. Clearance level classified."

In a few moments, Ari joined us in my laboratory, looking around as if curious about the layout. It gave her time to reacquaint herself with the disorientation of being in the presence of a non-human organism. It was a normal reaction to my appearance. Those people who were familiar with me, or those who had been prepped with a photograph still had to adjust to the reality of my presence. And repeat exposure, even at short intervals, doesn't diminish the need to process that reality.

I understood it. Years ago, the former Laboratory Director, Ignatius Cooper, had taken me aside after the disastrous meeting between my mother and me. I had requested it and had not considered that her reaction would not only be impersonal but that she would be unable to mask her registered disgust at the sight of her evolutionary creation. She had visibly flinched on the other side of the glass.

Ignatius had probably known how it was going to go down beforehand, but he was a great believer in self-determination, and he never was one to sugarcoat anything. "That's potentially as bad as it gets, I suspect," he told me. "But you need to resign yourself to the fact that it may be closer to the baseline reaction to your appearance than not. Humans are instinctual beings, even if they don't acknowledge such a thing. Once they become accustomed to you, it might get better, and it might not. It depends on the person. That is your reality. You don't have to react at all. I suggest this because it is the most intelligent and humane way to proceed."

Of course, he was right. If I feigned ignorance about what was happening, it blunted what came after.

When Ari's lizard brain settled down, she spoke first to Thida. "Dr. Rantha? I did not expect to find you on this side. I know you and Athes work closely together on many things, but especially now, with a viable embryo scheduled for implantation, I think it would be wiser to begin quarantine protocol as early as possible. AIDA, let Dr. Rantha back into her laboratory."

Thida nodded as if she had expected this, and AIDA let her cross into her lab space without security scanning. Thida's voice came over the intercom once she was opposite us at her workbench. "Athes, I will start prepping for new tissue samples. We can get started once your meeting is over. I'll schedule our teleconference with the doctors so we can discuss particulars for preparation."

"Thank you, Thida." I turned my attention back to my guest, who settled her gaze comfortably on my right shoulder. "I assume you received my report."

"I did. I did. I was hoping you could tell me what you were doing when these events occurred," Ari asked carefully.

"I was asleep. The noises coming from the subflooring awakened me, so I drained the tank and asked AIDA to perform a scan to identify the cause."

"Ram Vishnamurthy tells me his team was purging the saltwater pumps last night. They were performing the usual monthly maintenance. He thought perhaps the sound you heard was transmitted from the pumps," Ari supplied this information before I could ask a single question. Ram was Head of Engineering; his team was responsible for all mechanical aspects of the laboratory space.

"I did hear water moving, but no unusual machine noise. The sound was more like a disturbance, an air-water interface, and I thought something was moving through the water," I told her. "Was there a technician in the circuit while they did the purge?"

"Ah, I – think so," she answered slowly, nodding at the end to cover the lie. I knew if they were actively purging the pumps, it would be unsafe to have a diver in the system.

"And what about AIDA's finding that there was a non-resident bioorganism of the habitat present in the circuit?" I asked calmly.

"A glitch, we think," Ari lied again. She was terrible at it, and probably assumed that a lesser species like me was too primitive to catch it. "I think the programmers made the code so tight for your biome that anyone who lives in another zone of the habitat would be deemed a non-resident. Even if Thida – Dr. Rantha – were in the circuit, AIDA would identify her as a non-resident. You are especially important to this community, and the security of your biome is the utmost priority." She finished like the politician she was.

I said nothing, not planning to bring up the elephant in the room. Or the whale, either. Even if what Ari had told me were true, it didn't explain why AIDA had confirmed a finding that a non-human, humanoid lifeform had been present. I waited. The seconds ticked by. AIDA had turned off my music when the Director arrived, so the silence was almost a living thing.

Ari turned slightly and then stopped as if remembering something. "Oh, and we think that the bio read was off due to interference from the structure and the engineer's shielded wetsuit," she said, nodding. "Clearly, we need to tighten the parameters of the protocol and address failsafes so that these false readings don't continue to occur. You must have been terribly upset. I just want to reassure you that the programmers are expanding AIDA's directives to avoid such a result in the future."

"Well, thank you for coming in person, Director," I said. "It was kind of you. You could have just messaged me the information."

"Yes, well. We do consider you a V.I.P.," Ari confided, enunciating each letter in the acronym as though it were a separate word. "I needed to come down and check up on you. It's been too long, hasn't it?"

With that, she did turn her body away from me, but for form's sake, stayed another ten minutes making small talk and pretending to listen to a progress report on our recent work. She congratulated both of us on the viable embryo, making meaningful eye contact with 'Dr. Rantha' on the other side of the glass, and expressed her guarded enthusiasm for the development.

After she left, I internally congratulated myself for successfully giving away less than I had learned. But whatever I gleaned from her misdirection, I still had no satisfying answers. Other than giving Thida a significant look comprised of my raised brow folds once Ari was gone, I said nothing.

We worked in silence all morning, and the physicians had still not finalized their implantation protocol, which pushed the meeting back another day. I noticed when the genetic survey from the redistribution circuit dropped into my message cache but purposefully waited to look at it.

Thida turned on her music in the afternoon, loud and percussive, and she smiled at my startled expression when it came on. Her voice in my earpod was a surprise. "I don't understand why this doesn't appeal to you." I could hear the strain in her voice despite the teasing.

"This is why I have the ocean view," I told her, mimicking her lighthearted tone. "Your music would punch a hole in the dome."

She seemed reassured by my response, but there had been too many hours full of things too big to remain

unsaid. Sometime during the late morning, AIDA had
been instructed to generate the quarantine sequestration,
taking away Thida's clearance to cross over to my side of
the biome. I felt the loneliness then, and it surprised me.
I hadn't realized how much we had blurred the line that
was meant to exist between us, hadn't thought about
how we had erased certain boundaries.

After rations, I fed Triton and begged off. I told Thida I
needed sleep after the chaotic night I'd had and escaped
through the decomp chamber. Once inside, where my
command was unlikely to be overheard, I told AIDA to
lockdown my biome. "Restrict access, permission level
47AA1218, Athes, order expiry 06:00:00, or override
two conditions, 47AA1218, Athes return to lab or direct
countermand security."

That done, I knew that I would have no further
unannounced visitors. The only way to gain access to
my biome would be to override my instruction by
possessing a clearance level greater than mine. If Thida
could get in, it told me her clearance level exceeded
mine, and the activity missing from the log was removed
by order and not as she had described it to me the night
before. If she were unable to gain access, I would know
she had made an attempt because the act would trigger
request approval directly from me.

The tank was full, so AIDA flooded the small area after I
had removed my drysuit, and thus secured, I swam out
into the tank. I spent an hour swimming in an

elongated Mobius pattern along the long axis of the space. The biome was generous, considering space was at a premium, but I had to double back and move up and down to exercise properly.

An aquatic creature requires a tank volume of nearly four-hundredths of a cubic meter for every two-and-a-half centimeters of length, accounting for maximum potential growth whether or not the organism reaches that size. Triton, for example, had a potential lip to fin length of twenty centimeters, necessitating a volume just over three-tenths of a cubic meter, or roughly eight gallons of water to maintain an adequate habitat. That is a minimum; humane volume guidelines don't get published. I measure 1.83 meters in length, and I have done the math many times.

It, and an increasing number of other things around here, just don't add up the way they should.

Hovering vertically at the end of my swim, I brought my watch up to eye level, and punched in the code to direct the ArKive to send audio results of the genetic scan to my earpod. I closed my eyes and drifted in the water, listening carefully as the recording confirmed what AIDA had reported the night before. There was uncharacterized genetic material in the sample consistent with AIDA's initial report and my suspicions. I made a mental note to scrutinize the sequencing the next morning.

Then I succumbed to my exhaustion.

16

Screams are silent underwater.

The dream again, but it is a dream interrupted. I awaken, once again not knowing why I am awake. In my initial confusion, while letting go of the effects of sleep, I can sense that I am not alone in the tank.

I look around for Triton, who will often buzz my face when he seeks me out, but the darker shadow to my left is too large to be mistaken for a koi. I look again, unconvinced I am awake, realizing it is merely the dark expanse of the sea beyond the boundary wall.

I remain unsure about what has interrupted my sleep until AIDA's voice is in my earpod. "Acknowledge. 47AA1218 Athes. Aborted attempt to access water biome at 00:42:16, subject Rantha, Dr. Thida Ananya. Repeat notification, message number two."

I reaccess my watch to acknowledge receipt of notification, then stretch and try to clear away the grogginess and vestiges of the dream so I can concentrate. I am not sure what exactly I have learned. By aborting the request, the attempt did not test my theory about whether I could deny Thida entry. All it tells me is that she attempted to enter. The abort could have been to avoid alerting me to whether she could have overridden the security bar.

But I suspect the answer is not as complicated as I try to make it. If Thida's reasons for access were personal, she would ask permission. Lovers are respectful of autonomy, as are friends, siblings, colleagues, or any other person that recognizes equal standing in a relationship.

Only manipulation requires subterfuge.

17

But I cannot determine from recent events who is being manipulated. I consider Thida's reaction when I suggested she was compromised. Did she mistake my statement one of a concerned scientific colleague observing the demise of the clinical remove between us? Perhaps I felt she could no longer remain dispassionate about our work because of her feelings, and worry that our superiors would remove her from the project.

Or something else. A realization that the psychosocial experiment has backfired. That your partner recognizes your obfuscation and deceit.

Either way, that reaction was a type of admission. An acknowledgement that planning went on behind the scenes. Emotional approaches to me were considered and then discarded or deployed, whatever was thought best. That she was expected to contribute, sacrifice her aspirations for the future promise of career advancement. That she had conspired. That she had misread my responses to her less obvious overtures. That she had willingly agreed to manipulate me. That she had told them it was possible to do so.

She couldn't read my response to her kiss as indifference tempered with my curiosity about the lack of convincing passion. Her heart rate during the encounter never changed; I had recorded her telemetry from the time she entered the tank, felt her heart thumping against my torso during our embrace. The rate never topped seventy-four. No capillary flushing of the skin, no pupillary dilation.

Emotion has its own language, and it is embedded in physiologic response. Perhaps I am the villain, too cynical to ignore my training.

Perhaps she was not given a choice. A slippery argument, an option is always presented in some way or another. Just because one of the alternatives is less noxious does not negate the reality.

But of course, she was.

If nothing else, the timing was terrible in its singularity. A viable embryo after years of work, unexpected and vital. Triumphant even. But barely celebrated. All the years past, our coincident education, and pairing as research colleagues and cohabitators.

I could understand resetting the parameters of what is attractive to a human being over a few years of increasing familiarity. Still, desire does not take a decade to manifest, unless in the most antiquated of reasoning to allow my chronology to surpass some statutory threshold. I am reasonably convinced that Thida knows little of me other than what file number 47AA1218 can supply.

Never have I revealed motivation, ambition, yearning, or expectation. I assume our supervisors can build a working psychological construct regarding these attributes and approximate a personality profile based on my musical taste, reading list, and films I have viewed.

But they cannot, not ever, know what it is to lead an existence directed only by external motivation. My internal expectations cannot possibly be met. Where they are impossible is one avenue, the other deals with where they would create immediate conflict with the aims of my creator-captors.

They dangle bait. Don't pardon the pun. I do not require gratuitous physical pleasure; a lover foisted upon me gracelessly. Bait me with freedom, and with choice. But if those are only enticements, I serve myself poorly to become a puppet for them.

While I can stipulate that Thida has a human attractiveness, I had long ago decided that I was not seeking that kind of congress. I had a real need to determine who I was, and I am not sure that any being can do so without the benefit of others of their own kind. The false exchange of regard is entirely unfruitful.

The part of Thida that holds some empathy would remind me that if compromised, her replacement would remain on the other side of the glass. I would be treated like a specimen at best, with disdain or repugnance at worst. My mind, beauty, wit would be overlooked.

But an ugly truth has far greater value than the prettiest lie.

18

Without bothering to purge the tank, I do a wet decompress and emerge on the laboratory side of the glass. Triton's lips peek out from the ceramic skull sculpture in his tank that was repurposed from Aquarius Reef 7, the precursor to the final Aquaria build. I'm glad one of us is getting regular sleep.

"Play Leo Delibes' *Lakme, duet des fleurs,*" I request. It strikes me that the theme of the aria is oddly appropriate to the circumstance, dealing as it does with the relationship between two women who must depend upon one another to survive. Once the music has started, I call up the genetic survey results. "Show me ArKive data on genetic assay from water redistribution circuit."

"File not found. If message is in error, refine request for clarification."

"Genetic surveillance data request date 21K.12. Timestamp 05:32:46. Result summary, sequence focus DNA, cross-reference indeterminate species, non-resident, bioorganism."

"File does not exist. Unrecognized tags, cross-reference keys do not resolve the discrepancy."

I tried to access the results that I knew I had confirmed only hours prior but to no avail. Frustrated, I reviewed the log cache to find the flag I had placed, but it had been altered. The events of the first six hours of the previous day were no longer detailed, and a long bracket spooled across the cache. The details of the event, the event itself, had been redacted from the record.

It bothered me, but I had my own ideas about what was happening, so I put that aside for a moment. It was their way to curtail further questions.

I sat for fully twenty minutes, listening to the crescendoing voices looping over and around me, a ballet of sound, motionless otherwise, considering what gains I could make without accepting a certain amount of risk. None.

Which is how I found myself standing at the door to Thida's lab. Leaving the music playing, I said the following, not entirely sure it would work. Recent events had further called into question what, if anything, I could believe.

"Ignore, security protocol, all doors, habitat biome zones A and B. Ignore, log directives. Ignore, bioscan parameters, critical exception tissue bank, and nursery. Duration end mark 21K.13.05:05:05." I wanted a deadline that would be easy to read on my watch.

I don't pray. I just closed my eyes and let the voices transport me once more for courage. I shed my drysuit while I was completing the internal debate. The door opened when I approached it, and then I was through to the other side and committed to whatever came next.

My reading of the blueprints was fresh in my mind, and once in Thida's sleeping quarters, I found the redistribution access hatch without difficulty. It was in the far corner of the bathroom suite, not flush with the floor panel like in the tank; it had a raised hatch that opened on a hinge.

It was round, like a bulkhead door, smaller and modified so that it could be opened and shut from above or below. It opened readily enough but was heavier than I expected, and I cradled it as I lifted it, taking time to settle it without making noise that might wake Thida.

The water below was dark, impenetrably so, which gave me pause. It should not have surprised me, there was no light source beneath the habitat, and the redistribution circuit was a series of pipes, closed off save for their egress to the open water. It was moving slightly, up and down, likely reflecting the force of the ocean current.

I had a decision to make, and quickly, as my skin was drying out, and with the loss of water went my ability for respiration. I gripped the wheel for support as I slid into the water, dogging the hatch carefully behind me. I was not sure what I felt initially other than cold. The water was freezing, but it didn't take long before that concern receded with the realization that what I was doing was potentially extremely dangerous. I had never been outside the biome; I had no understanding or development of any natural instincts about this environment.

And the darkness was complete, impenetrable, and disorienting. I reached up to feel for the hatch, but I had already drifted some distance from it, and I felt only the smooth metal skin of the pipe vault above me. It had a slimy consistency that I could not immediately characterize. The motion of my arm stirred up some bioluminescent algae, which provided a brief glimpse of the diameter of the tube, but also reminded me of the light feature on my watch, which I activated.

The light allowed me to see about two meters ahead and behind me, and thankfully showed me the hatch I had come through. I scrutinized the underside, memorizing the number. Behind me was a T-junction turn that I guessed was where the circuit met the reef rock to the rear of the habitat. There was no other apparent marine life present, which confused me. I revisited the feel of the slimy walls of the duct and guessed that perhaps whatever had been used to treat the conduit retarded the ability of marine life to take hold in the circuit.

Ahead of me was an indeterminate length of straight pipe, so I swam forward and found what I assumed was the access point below my tank. The blind square of metal had been welded shut, but here, on the outside, there was a bolt to which a dog wheel could easily be remounted should it need to be modified in the future.

I backtracked to the T-junction and turned right. I followed the tube, swimming more quickly and noticing that I was adapting to the temperature, something I could not have readily predicted. I did not think it a byproduct of distraction; I felt warmer, as if my blood were being redistributed to my skin and subcutaneous tissue as I swam.

I ignored the junctions that I passed, assuming they were access routes to individual biomes, following a main 'racetrack' around the perimeter, enjoying the relative freedom of flying along in the pipes.

As I turned the second corner, nearing what I assumed would correspond with the ocean side of the redistribution circuit, rather than shoot down another corridor to the far corner, I reached a large opening, wide, fluted, and flattening. My momentum was arrested here because the prevailing force was pushing and pulling from the open water.

As I approached the mouth of the intake, I noticed increasing marine encroachment and almost did not realize that I had exited the duct and was floating in the ocean. I turned back, seeing the reef through new eyes, with no barrier.

I gently kicked myself upward, my light reflecting off the glass of one of the minidomes jutting out just above my head. I followed the curve of the glass, able to see into the habitat, the sleeping scientist less than two meters away, the lab beyond, and then seeing it all from above as I floated up to the reef architecture running onward to the land shelf above me somewhere, obscured in darkness.

I didn't go any farther, not wanting to lose my bearings, but spent some time contemplating the busy machinations of the macro life that lived here. Many creatures that I had assumed I would never come closer to than my holo screen were sharing my immediate environment. I could interact with them even more closely than I could with Triton.

Initially, many of them darted away, out of the light, and away from my shadow as it crept over the reef. But I held still and tucked my hands under my arms and hovered, observing without interfering. I knew what it was to be the fish in the tank; it would be the ultimate hypocrisy to misbehave in such a way.

I turned back, still facing my unanswered questions. I drifted back down, over the reef, the dome and its sleeping inhabitants, and back to the intake and onward, completing the circuit. This time I followed every junction, searched every channel.

I relocated the hatch beneath Thida's sleeping quarters and was just about to climb back up when I had an idea. I swam the handful of meters to the blind entry below my tank and examined it one more time. A glance at my watch told me it was just after four-thirty.

I hovered a few moments more, purposefully scraping up the slime near my hatch and holding it in my mouth for safekeeping, then swam back to the other hatch. The slime had an acrid, chemical tang, and I realized that I was taking quite a risk. It was gelatinous as well, but other than the horrible taste, it seemed to have no immediate ill effects.

I managed to wrench the wheel with enough force to get it open, but pushing it up proved a challenge until I thought to put my feet down on the bottom of the conduit pipe and stand, shouldering the weight as I did so. It was enough to allow me to wiggle through.

I closed both hatch and cover and then used a towel to dry the water that had splashed on the tile. I was careful to choose the one from the highest shelf, in the corner, making sure it was folded and put back in place as though it had not been used.

I hurried back across to my side of the lab, retrieved a small beaker, and spat the slime from the redistribution circuit into it; adding water and gently swirling it made it appear to be a water sample. I shrugged into my drysuit and returned to Thida's dwelling.

19

I stood watching her sleep and didn't bother to leave when her alarm sounded at precisely ten minutes of five. She woke promptly, sat up, and did a delayed double-take when she realized that she was exactly where she expected to be, but I was not.

"But…how…did you?" Thida managed to ask, still half asleep, peering at me through one open eye.

"You taught me," I replied, as if it were obvious.

She looked confused for a moment and then remembered the confidences of her visit to the tank two nights prior.

"I have to assume that some of what you tell me is true," I added, ignoring her hurt expression when the statement hit its intended target.

"Athes," she began, but seeing my expression, she stopped. She flopped onto her back and studied the ceiling. "I needed you to trust me."

I kept silent, answer enough.

"Why did you say that to me yesterday? That they knew I was compromised?" she said suddenly, never taking her eyes from the curving dome above us.

"Aren't you?" I challenged her.

"I don't know why you'd say it," Thida replied testily. "I chose this assignment. I wanted it. I knew how important it was, and when I got to know you, I realized you deserved to be happy. I told the directors as much. I understood how important it was for you to have a partner who would look out for your interests."

"Does that include seducing me?" I asked, in the most direct tone I could manage. It drew her attention off the ceiling.

"It includes whatever they think you need," she said quietly, and I was impressed that she could maintain eye contact for the few seconds that she managed it, understanding that she was found out.

"What I want should be simple to guess and certainly easy to arrange," I told her. "But I am not free. Our relationship is not balanced. No matter how this happens or doesn't, humans will continue to hold any one of my kind that survives as a captive. It will never be enough to have relief that you can evolve; your species will always want to control and direct that evolution.

"What happens if the day comes when there are more of us than you? Will the amphibious have to resort to bloody revolt to gain their freedom? From a species that escaped to a place for which it has no adaptation. Would those like me be used to reduce the risks humans have to face in the sea? Where we are exposed to keep you safe, to keep the dangers of the aquatic world from intruding upon what you have built.

"Have you forgotten your history? Or perhaps you are just ignoring it. Hoping I would be lulled into believing humans had changed. That the wise fish would be grateful she was such a precious commodity that she had to be protected from the one thing that would make her equal, that would make her free?"

I looked at my watch. Two minutes past five.

"I should have known it when you showed up, suggesting that we had real privacy. But now I know that you will be privy to whatever lies they will choose to weaponize to get me to perform. And if I thought you would tell me the truth, I would ask the critical question, but I fear that we are out of time."

20

The quiet in the lab that morning should have seemed merciful, but it just seemed ominous.

I crossed into the tank biome to take a swim at midday, mostly to avoid any conversation with Thida during ration distribution.

I had forgotten about everything other than my grief. My watch reminded me of the engineering schedule, so I wasn't surprised when Jesús came swimming up to the glass. It was a bright day; water visibility was good. A school of red emperors drifted down behind him and disappeared across the reef, hunting for food.

I struggled through the niceties of small talk before I gave it up. I turned away in the middle of Jesús' question, not wanting him to ask me what was wrong. But he knocked on the glass, so I turned back, and he repeated it, *what's wrong?*

Rather than answer, I signed my own question. I asked whether he had ever seen another creature like me, either out on the reef or somewhere near the habitat.

His hesitation was his answer. His eyes told me that he would not lie to me. He was my friend. But his hands never moved again, and soon he was gone.

For company during the afternoon, I listened to the telemetry of 74ZQ5837. Determined, strong, steady. Blissful and advantaged in its ignorance.

I logged the water sample from the subfloor circuit pipe for analysis and dutifully completed my other tasks. I fed Triton and decided to skip evening rations, which earned me a warning from AIDA.

"Ration maintenance ensures inhabitant health and integrity. Nutrient and micronutrient deficits can result in-"

"Bite me."

"Unrecognized command. Ration maintenance ensures…"

"Override warning message. Open decompression bay door, laboratory side. Dry decompression protocol."

I was too listless to do much swimming, and I was sure sleep would never find me. But it did.

When the dreams woke me, I had some difficulty shaking them off, slow to fully reach consciousness. A small sound in my ear persisted, and for a few moments, I thought I must still be dreaming.

But the sound went on and on, a small beacon in my earpod. It was an alert of some kind, but I'd heard it only rarely, perhaps in system testing. I glanced out toward the lab and saw Triton floating belly up in his tank. I swam over to the glass to get a better look. He was dead.

The beeping in my ear was continuous now, and I made the connection slowly because whatever had killed Triton was causing the biome's water sensors to alarm continuously.

"God damn it, AIDA. Stop this. It's killing her…God damn you all…" Thida's voice was in my earpod, along with others, whose voices were less distinct and not as recognizable.

My last thought before the darkness closed over my head was that I had to get out of the tank. They had murdered my fish.

  But it wasn't the worst they could do. I was about to learn that.

21

When next I woke, I was in the examination pod. I had no way to determine how much time had passed. I tried to look at my watch but could not lift my arm. Or my head. I didn't feel well.

Salt crusts ringed my nostrils, and my lower torso was numb. I took inventory of myself, provisionally reassured that I could still wiggle my toes and fingers. Weakly.

"Mist," I whispered, and thankfully my voice command was loud enough for AIDA to respond, filling the pod with cool spray. I felt marginally better. "Time?"

"21K.27.16:23:15," AIDA responded promptly.

There was movement on Thida's side of the lab, and the figure that came close to the pod was initially only a shadow beyond the lights.

"Lights down." I heard the command, but it was not Thida's voice that gave it. I turned my eyes toward it and saw Ari Lipton looking down at me, her expression a mixture of triumph and disgust. "I see you're awake."

"…kept me asleep for two weeks?" I think I managed to get most of the question out coherently.

"Yes. Well. We thought it safest to induce a coma to ensure your cooperation with the necessary therapeutic interventions leading up to your implantation date. It was successful, by the way." Her gaze flicked over to the monitors and back to my face.

I turned my head to see the heads-up display on the pod wall. Telemetry tracings for two organisms, one mine, slowed by drugs, the other, much more rapid, but still steady and strong. Two of us in the pod. 74ZQ5837 was now a part of me.

Ari responded to my expression of surprise and outrage. I hoped she could not see my fear. "I was always willing to let you operate under the illusion of consent, but once you demonstrated to us that you might exercise your will against our best interests, I decided to drop the pretense."

"Finally, we can have an honest… conversation…" I managed, enjoying the way her forehead wrinkled in anger, happy I was evoking a response.

"Right, then. We'll continue the chemical restraints," Ari said. I couldn't move my head enough to see what she did inside the glove box, but she made sure that the jab of the needle into my flank was rough and painful, that I would feel it before the darkness came down again.

When next I came to my senses, I asked for the time once more.

"Request denied," was AIDA's abrupt response.

"Mist," I said, and this time, thankfully, was rewarded with water. I repeated the request three times in succession before the relative humidity in the examination pod was high enough for me to breathe more easily.

This time no one came at the sound of my voice, so I assumed it was late. Or exceedingly early. The lights were down on both sides of me, Nocturne protocol. I felt slightly less groggy than before, so I hoped that meant that less time had elapsed. It was horrifying not to know how long I had been under this time.

I moved my arm a bit to try and discern whether my watch was still in place. I did manage to lift my hand enough to see that they had taken that as well. I considered this.

"Locate personal data device."

"Request denied."

I thought about this for a moment. There had to be a workaround. I struggled to get my brain to work. Thinking was making it hurt. Thinking was making everything hurt.

"Telemetry to audible," I requested. Hearing those two heartbeats creating their own symphony had the effect I was hoping for. It was a much-needed distraction that became meditative in its monotony. With that soothing backdrop, I could consider my situation.

"Locate ghost, personal data device, audio file, 21K.12." I hoped that the log cache scrubbing had failed to retrieve and delete the smaller file requested to my device that morning, and I was rewarded for my creative thinking. I still wanted to compare the nonresident organism's DNA to my own.

"Ghost located." AIDA, if I could fist bump something right now, it might even be you.

"Ignore, conversation log, this instance. Ignore, reporting transcript and security check. Ignore, subject of execution command. Play file, skip to result comparison to DNA 47AA1218, cross reference markers to unknown bioorganism, and integrate findings." Once AIDA had provided me with the confirmation that what I had only suspected was, in fact, true, there was one more task needed to hide it in plain sight.

"Ignore, conversation log, this instance. Ignore, reporting transcript and security check. Ignore, subject of execution command. Place ghost in music file and append to terminus of Leo Delibes' *Lakme, Duet des fleurs.*"

The audio data would play for whomever next listened to the file, and I hoped it would count for something. By asking AIDA to ignore both commands, I was buying time, as neither execution would be noted on the log cache. There would be no record of my latest mischief.

I was shocked that the override was still working. Perhaps I could use it to save my life.

22

Each time I awakened, I felt worse. I had never gone more than twelve hours without total immersion, and now, I had been kept in the examination pod for weeks.

There were open sores on my skin, and they didn't appear to be healing. My heart rate was slowing, but thankfully, 74ZQ5837 seemed to suffer no ill effects from the decline of its host.

Dr. Lipton and I traded insults. Hers were cruelly creative, and as I weakened, they affected me more. I knew she only had to keep me alive until 74ZQ5837 was viable, and it was unlikely I would live a day beyond that event horizon.

I tormented her by turning on the music in the lab. "Play Leonard Cohen's *Hallelujah*," I told AIDA once, shortly after I had awakened and confirmed that the Director was present. "It's Triton's favorite." Ah, my private, cynical amusements. Lipton hated it.

She retaliated by disparaging 74ZQ5837 when she knew I could hear. "Let's not bother to give *it* a name. And make a note that we should harvest anything salvageable from the host in case we need tissue for the clone."

My death was assured. It became increasingly difficult to get enough moisture, and when I was conscious, I was increasingly subject to reflexive airless gasps for breath; my bad dreams had become my reality.

From this terrible perspective, I wondered why I had ever returned from my ocean escape. Still protecting what was not mine, what would never belong to me. I could not protect the infant growing inside me. I could only hope its life would be better than mine, but I was unable to sustain any illusion that even approximated faith in such a farfetched idea.

23

I dream of Thida's voice.

"You're not dreaming. I'm here," she says, and I realize
I must have said something out loud. "Open your
eyes."

I do, and she is seated beside the examination pod, a
look of anguish and worry on her face. A deep wrinkle
runs between her brows.

"It's worse than I thought," I observe, and see a ghost of
a smile on her face. "How are you here?"

"Shhhh. I managed to convince the directors that they
can count on me to be here to represent their interests,"
she tells me softly. "That I am a team player." But I
have been reading Thida's expressions for years, and
now it tells me she is decidedly not on their team.

"Just this once, tell me the truth, okay?" My request
manages to evoke a smile this time, a real one, no half
measures.

"They are killing you, half accidentally and half
purposefully, I think," she tells me.

"Are you certain about those ratios?" I ask, trying
desperately to stay awake for her sake.

"Just stop trying to be so funny and try harder to live," she suggests, putting a finger to her lips to stop me from saying more. "AIDA, seal examination pod, and fill." I hear a vacuum noise, and the pod begins to fill with water, converting it to a tank. I had no idea it could do that, but there is no more time to consider this because I am too weak to remain conscious.

Instead of insults, I came round to Thida's soft touch, tending my skin. More water and fewer drugs had me feeling stronger, but I needed to swim.

"I'm not allowed to let you out of the pod. I can't keep telling you no, so don't ask. It is hard enough as it is."

"Tell me why Lipton would give up the opportunity to continue tormenting me?" I ask, genuinely interested in the answer.

She shrugged. "Your responses didn't make it fun enough? I think she thought you would cry and beg. She was working harder than she wanted to and not being rewarded with enough psychic gain," Thida said matter of factly. She sighed and turned her eyes to the ceiling.

"Why didn't you visit me more often? Before, I mean," I asked her. "I wondered that it didn't bother you not to see the ocean."

"I'm afraid of it," she said, as if reading my mind. "I didn't mind living along the inner corridor. I didn't want to see the ocean. I wanted to pretend that we don't have to live down here, under the water."

"That's an interesting position, all things considered," I replied. Thida's words made me even sadder than before. "What are *they* going to think about this conversation?"

"If they even bother to listen, I don't care," she said.

One day, after draining the pod so that she could attend my healing skin, she paused with a gasp as she slid her hands through the glove ports.

"Athes, look – may I?" she pointed to my belly, which was becoming noticeably curved. I reached up and guided her gloved hands to my abdomen, placing them over the baby. Her face lit with wonder, and I just watched her. Her happiness was a gift. And just as suddenly, she withdrew, unable to hide her tears before she managed to escape out of my field of view. She fled the lab and did not come back.

After that, several days passed without any indication she would ever return. An efficient, brisk medical technician was dispatched to provide my care. He was surprisingly young, spoke short sentences to me only when it was unavoidable. At least he did not protest when I asked AIDA to play music.

Though my physical health had improved, my emotions did not make much of a recovery. I had stopped tracking time and had nothing to look forward to. I missed my daily routine, missed solving problems in the lab. Missed the biome tank, and Triton, and anything else that could not be returned to me. The only thing I was moving toward in the future was my death.

One morning, AIDA greeted me as the daytime lights came up in the lab. "Congratulations, Athes. It is a beautiful day for a birthday."

24

I had entirely forgotten that it was approaching. Likely my last.

The health technician was late, and I worried as the day wore on. It was late afternoon before I heard the muffled sounds of AIDA opening the outer door. Then nothing. I could sense activity on Thida's side of the lab. It sounded like something was happening in her sleeping quarters, but I couldn't be sure.

Then I heard Thida's voice; it sounded as though she were giving AIDA complicated instructions.

It seemed a long time before she approached the pod. She glanced in at me, and I could see that she had been crying. She said nothing, just opened the chamber.

"Are you strong enough to climb out?" she asked, but she was already pulling me to the opening. I sat up first and was pleased that I was not too dizzy to stand. Which I managed, all the while with Thida under my arm and moving with more urgency than I had ever seen.

"Something's happened," I asked, but it wasn't really a question. I understood what motivated Thida; all our years together had taught me something.

She didn't bother to answer at first. Then, softly, she said, "It's your birthday."

"Not just mine," I said, wondering how she would react. She stood very still for several moments and then pivoted gently to help me sit down on the nearby stool.

"How long?" she wonders, and I am not even sure she is asking me a question. "How long have you known?"

"I suspected when AIDA confirmed that there was a non-resident humanoid present in the redistribution circuit. I knew when I was able to trick AIDA into comparing the genetic sampling to my own DNA, sometime after the implantation. There were also cells in the chemical coating lining the pipe. I–" I stopped before I said too much, thinking I was caught, but Thida was still too distracted by my discovery to notice.

She looked at me with newfound respect. "There are two of you. In-vitro frequently results in multiparous births."

"I'm the control subject," I said suddenly, wanting to spare hearing the science I already knew, not wanting any more subterfuge. "One to live in a human habitat, the other to the sea."

"You're not the control." Thida shook her head. "She is. Put into the ocean at birth. No assistance for food, vitamins, education, medical treatment, no land-based intervention, no protection from elements or predators. For many years it was assumed she had died. Engineering started reporting sightings about three years ago. They trapped her, brought her in, took samples. All kinds. And then sent her back out. But not before they 'told' her about you. She has no developed spoken language skills, so they can't really measure her level of communication. They showed her your living quarters here in the dome. Let her watch you from the open water."

"No assistance, no intervention, full disclosure," I marveled.

"While you had every advantage they could think to afford you, every intervention, and no disclosure," Thida told me.

"She was trying to visit me," I marveled.

"For a long time, she was trying to get in. They had sealed the hatch when they built your biome tank but had to strip the handle from it," Thida clarified. "It was a near miracle that you only discovered the disturbance the one time you finally did."

"Where is she now?" I ask, finding enthusiasm I haven't felt in some time, if ever. "There's no point in keeping us apart anymore."

"Athes, 74ZQ5837 is actually *her* clone. When she was initially captured, her gonadal cells were harvested to increase the possibility of having the greatest number of viable embryos. They were pooled with your cells but separated by series so that we would know which one of you created the clone, so that the studies done on the new baby would benefit from data about the lifestyle and diet of its progenitor organism.

"It may not have been a coincidence that she tried to gain access to the biome that night. It is possible that she was no longer interested in getting to you. You played the telemetry of the embryo. The psychologists have suggested that she may have been attracted to it by some maternal instinct that we don't understand." After Thida finished, the silence felt like a weight.

"You haven't answered my question," I said softly.

"She is missing," Thida told me.

"She is dead," I said, convinced of its truth.

"Likely. She jeopardized their plans for continuing the lie."

"Can you live with that?" I challenged her.

"I can't prove anything. I guess I have to."

"You can't prove her death?" I asked, incredulous.

"No, Athes, I cannot prove she existed. They kept no record of her. None that I am aware of anyway," Thida's voice broke, and although I suspected she did know more than she was telling me, she had paid enough. She couldn't bring the dead to life.

25

We sat in silence for several moments. Finally, Thida stood and reached out a hand.

"Come. Can you walk? I don't want you to dry out."

I smiled. "I get to swim?"

"It is your birthday," she replied, but her smile was too small for one granting a gift. Her statement was unhappy, somehow.

I allowed her to assist me, turning toward the door to the opposite lab and the tank biome, but she pulled me gently in the other direction, to the back of the habitat and into her living quarters. She led me into the bathroom suite and over to the open hatch. The water bobbed up and down gently at the base of the opening.

"So, your security clearance was higher than mine all along," I observed with mock disappointment, and she smiled, but didn't answer.

I sat on the edge of the opening and put my feet in the water. "What was her name?" I asked.

"Aquana. Aquarius and Diana. Resourceful fish," Thida replied. "Are you sure you can swim?"

I didn't answer her question. She reached down and settled my earpod in my ear.

"Some music for the journey?" she asked.

"AIDA, play Leo Delibes' *Lakme, duet des fleurs*," I said, then to Thida, "Promise me you'll listen to the very end."

26

The music followed me to the intake, and I could still hear it as I cleared the dome of the biome refuge I had shared with Thida.

When the signal faded out, I removed the earpod and let it fall away.

I swam on, over the shoulder of the reef, until I could look back and see no trace of Aquaria. No trace of any human interference in this beautiful place. The sunlight penetrated the depths, sparking points of luminescence off the scales of the iridescent fish that danced over the coral.

And the nature of the silence was awe-inducing. For the first time, I understood that feeling that Jesús had tried to describe to me. How the sea held him, and its quiet claimed him. Something in me loosened and let go, and I realized it was my fear.

I didn't need it anymore. I was where I belonged. Free.

Doppelganger

I stumble onward.

The cold wind carries slivers of ice that threaten to blind me.

Something, perhaps only shadow, moves at the periphery of my vision. I blink against the elements and swipe my glove impatiently across my eyes, hoping it will go away. Instead, the shadows multiply – and where there was one, there are now many.

*They slink along several meters away, safely out of reach. But they **are** there. Stalking me.*

*No hallucination this. My brain is fine. Well, mostly. Years ago, I might have been worried about the possibility of a psychotic break. Perhaps because **before** it was the worst thing I could imagine. A nightmare.*

Back then, we didn't know the meaning of nightmare. But we learned, in the only way that humans often do.

The hard way.

1

The organisms must be xenomorphs. Not like the ones in the old *Alien* movies from the late 20th century. Perhaps that's fortunate. But no less devastating.

A xenomorph is simply an organism that can adapt its form in a multitude of ways, perhaps in a limitless number of ways. From an evolutionary standpoint, perfect, because it can change as it needs to in order to survive a number of environmental insults.

From an evolutionary standpoint, deadly, especially if it is a predator, because any ecosystem into which it is introduced will succumb to its supremacy. If that sounds familiar, it bloody should.

On Earth, the best example of such a creature would be humans. But we are limited, dimorphic, hopelessly bogged down by evolution, our forms, our adaptations relatively glacial in pace. We certainly set in motion a chain of events that would alter our ecosystem, but we were never going to survive those alterations as a species.

If our atmospheric composition changed by less than five percent, we could not adapt in time to survive. The xenomorph apparently accomplishes even more extreme changes in the time it takes one of us to change our underwear.

Which means they are like a locust swarm on a planet like Earth. And humans the young crop, vulnerable and unprotected. I think these xenomorphs have done this before, many times. They are the ultimate galactic colonizers. World–enders.

These are all simply my assumptions, because there is no way to know for sure. No science to back them up. But these statements are based on observable facts, and my observations are probably the largest compilation of data. Not that they can be reproduced to be sure. Or shared. The hallmarks of research. I won't be giving any TED talks on the subject. I'm too busy trying to survive.

2

I assume the devastating traits of these aliens are what most people succumbed to in the beginning. I am sure that several others must have died at the hands of their fellow humans, when resources became scarce, and the concept of survival of the fittest was put to the test.

The news never covered it, but I noticed. I noticed faces were changing, and I wasn't seeing any I recognized anymore. After that, I was only seeing myself.

I was already sick when they came. I had admitted my headaches to my physician, had started treatment for the nosebleeds. Was a bad patient, but then, who isn't? I was busy at work, and who doesn't procrastinate about seeing more doctors. And then, in the aftermath, what finished it was the end of humanity.

It happened quickly, because we are desperately social beings; seeing another human, especially once it became rare, was the cruel and deadly trap laid for us.

And which human face comforts us most? For this, there is reliable science. Our own face. Why? Because it is the one we see the most often from birth to death, at least owing to the presence of mirrors, that is. We don't even have to be particularly narcissistic for this to be true. We have subconsciously catalogued our own faces down to the tiniest detail, making it the most recognizable one each individual will ever know.

Consider why most of us have a problem with photos of ourselves. Bothersome really. We see them and we don't like the way we look. Something is off. Obviously the picture is a reproduction of our appearance. But it is not the one we are accustomed to seeing. Mirrors again are the culprit.

When you see your face, over and over, day after day, year after year, you are memorizing a reflection, the literal reverse of what is actually there. And as we are not perfectly symmetrical beings, this is what we seize upon when we see our own photograph. It looks wrong, not because it isn't us, rather because it is the actual, the opposite of what we are familiar with, what comforts us.

And this is the reason why our friends and family tell us that the picture is wonderful; they cannot see what we see. The image in the reproduction has the face they are used to looking upon, it does not upset the balance of a comfortable reality.

The xenomorphs have exploited this ruthlessly. They could change their appearance to mirror their victim. Seeing yourself causes a moment of hesitation. And that hesitation is what could cost me my life.

Any longer exposure to the creature and the facsimile organism has tells. These things don't move right. I suspect that the species was never bipedal. Or hell, maybe they were, but our gravity is different enough from theirs to make the exercise awkward.

I'll bet it was worst for the idents, those twins that look alike. Or perhaps better. Used to seeing your double,

you embrace them, right? Not knowing you are
embracing death. Most of them probably never knew
what was happening to them. The smallest of mercies.

And the xenomorphs have no memory for this mimicry,
these simulacra. Once their target is dead, they need to
take on the appearance of the next victim, and the next.
Eventually, these things will probably all just have the
same face.

Which is good for me. They won't show up looking like
my dead father or my ex-lover. Nope. Just me.

So if I see myself, I know it's on. My enemy wears *my*
face. There's something poetic about it really, something
deeply philosophical. Existential even.

Damn moon. That angled shadow created by your glow is behind me, moving, caught in my peripheral vision it seems to show me a stalking spectre, someone or something silently reaching for me among these dark trees.

In the glow of the streetlamps or carriage lights it is worse. See there? My shadow is obvious, right where it should be. But then moonlight grants another that is insubstantial, hallucinatory, causing me to question whether I am followed. No. Just shadowed, paced by the disappearing double, now here and then gone.

Perhaps a metaphor, a manifestation of a shadowy conscience, a straw man for my guilt.

3

I remember that first day, coming home. The headache was bad that time, I had left work, just wanted to get to a quiet, dark place. I recall sitting in my car in the driveway for a time, overcoming the nausea. That throbbing behind my eyes always the worst part of it.

I think I may have even passed out for a time. Blacked out, really. Lost time. The sun had moved in the sky by the time I hauled myself out of the seat. It was alarming, I could not remember coming home.

At the door, someone looking out. My face, oddly blurred, doubled by the effect of seeing my reflection in the cutout window by the entry as it layered over the face peering out. The front door saved me, that moment when my confusion and fear galvanized me.

That barrier gave me time to prepare to defend myself. Because it moved, or something about the migraine made me hallucinate, but the vision seemed to waver or melt before solidifying once more.

I should have run, back to the car, back out and away. But I was overcome by a sort of righteous anger, an instinct to defend my home. I opened the door, and pushed my key into its (*my*) eye, using this forward momentum to knock the creature over. The blood was all over me.

Then, Jamie's softball bat in the umbrella stand beside the door. I remember reaching for it, and I can still hear my sobs in my dreams. The broken, bloodied thing when I was through, my frenzied swings, so ineffectual when trying to hit a ball, served me better in defense of my life. I blacked out, surely from the trauma of it, or the necessity, the crescendo of pain in my own splitting skull.

When I came to, I was lying there where I had fallen, but the creature was gone. The front door open to the darkness beyond. I heard a familiar sound outside, and stumbled out. The car, dinging insistently that someone had left something unsecured. The driver side door was open, the keys in the ignition. There were a few drops of blood in the seat. The rearview mirror revealed a frightful visage. The telltale signs of a nosebleed but no other evidence of the battle I had fought.

Nor could I find any evidence of a body. Had they taken it? And why not me? Had they thought me already dead there on the floor? The only evidence of violence was the smeared gore at the doorway. So little on my clothing.

My arms and shoulders ached for three days.

It became a pattern I lived with. They were neat in their kills; their victims disappeared without a trace. Insidious. I learned that I couldn't afford to let them get that close again, the physical cost was too great.

And I didn't need to, thanks to Jamie. I knew how to honor his memory. I would kill as many as I could.

I wouldn't have to get close. I had his crossbows.

4

I have to go out to replenish supplies, and I forage for non-perishable food items in the other houses nearby.

They are all empty, their residents long since taken or killed by the xenomorphs. I only do these interior searches during daylight hours.

I won't give the xenomorphs shadows from which to ambush me.

If I have to go abroad at night, I stay in the open, so I can see them approaching.

The cardinal isn't red anymore, his feathers dulled in color, a sickly hue that is neither orange nor pink. He flings himself against the transom window with fighting force, attacking the foe he sees there, alas, his rival is his own reflection.

To him it is a threat that could cost him his territory, a dying poisonberry tree, and his aging mate.

Or perhaps he too knows the world is ending.

5

We used to joke about it. I was never strong enough to fire the recurves or compounds, but the crossbow only required the strength to lock it.

Jamie preferred the upright bow, preferred the need for strength and concentration to fire it. He said it made the advantage he had over the deer when hunting much smaller; it humbled him. He hated those who hunted for sport, called it a waste.

I could even load the crossbow ahead of time; he had shown me how to pull the line out and brace the frame with my feet. I had just enough leverage to cock it. I didn't have to be strong enough to hold it, as my bow had a release.

I kept it loaded near the windows facing the rear of the house. The hill sloped away in back, creating an elevation on the main floor, which gave me an advantage if anything approached from the woods.

And they tried; one climbed up onto the deck outside the kitchen. The arrow's force carried it over the railing. I ventured out with a carving knife in case it wasn't dead, but ominously, I found no sign of it.

I wonder about my sanity. I feel as though I am losing time, sometimes only an hour here and there, other times a day. Conscious memory is a slippery thing, it flows and evades capture. I cannot patch together an entire day since it all began, and I wonder if the apocalyptic isolation is stripping me of reason.

Today, returning from foraging for summer berries, I discovered the front door ajar — had I left it open? Sometimes the wind can push it if the latch is not secure.

Quiet inside, but I wasn't alone. Pay attention to how a dwelling feels, and you will know whether other beings are about. All my internal alarms put me on my guard.

I went through the dining room, a superstitious ploy, a diversion, if one were needed, since I usually went the more direct route around the stairs, through the great room. The advantage of the latter a direct view through to the kitchen, which might give any adversary the same line of sight to me. The advantage of the former, stealth.

I stepped out of my boots on the porch, and stepped inside, silently and carefully. I slid across the polished parquet in the entryway and onto the carpeted floor next to the piano, reaching across quietly to the music stand to drop it down into place. I let it land on my fingers and held it, exposing the hunting knife I had secreted there.

Its weight was comforting in my hand as I crept onward, avoiding disturbing the chair at the corner of the dining table with my hip, which seemed to have been my repeated habit.

There was a juvenile deer in my kitchen. Too, too docile. Not bothering to look for a way out. Just standing there. Its head turned toward me when I appeared in the doorway. Beautiful. Those brown eyes

mesmerizing, peaceful. Its movements wrong. No grace.
No bounding flight of escape.

A trap. But for whom?

I watched my reflection on the shiny blank expanse of its
eye. Closer. It made a small sound when the knife went
in, familiar somehow, like a lament, or an apology.

Once should have been enough but it was moving; those
kicks can be fatal. I had trouble retrieving the blade at
first, but then, a rhythm – unnecessary. But then, self-
preservation can become a compulsion requiring of its
own symphony.

Bloodbath. A word for movies, crime scenes. An
abstraction before. I have learned that as a descriptor it
leaves nothing to be desired. So much of it, drying black
on every surface. But no body – where? Did it go? Was
it taken while I was – but no, I never left, never turned
away?

What has happened to me? I have been alone too long
with my memories, and I have lost the ability to preserve
them somehow. It is as if who I am now is stranded here,
the bloody tide carries who I was further and further from
the shore.

And why was the deer a deer? Why mimic something
new, why not keep wearing my face? Unless the deer
was a metaphor?

Was the deer a dear?

Funny thing, now I know I can handle them one on one. I wonder what will happen if they ever decide to work together and come for me as a group?

So many preparations to make; so many traps to set.

The headaches are worse.

Crippling at times.

Exacerbated by the smell-stench of death. It is everywhere now; I cannot escape it. It comes from the surrounding houses, although when I forage I find no corpses.

It is on the air, a constant reminder of this planetary graveyard. The miasma has seeped into the taste of the water from the well, and it has crept onto my clothing, up my nose. It is in my pores. I cannot scrub it away.

Putrescence. Perhaps I too, have finally succumbed. Dead.

How would I know?

It isn't as if there is anyone who could tell me.

Neurosurgical Consultation (Excerpt with Redactions)

CC: Lancaster County District Attorney

MR# 773121819

PATIENT: (redacted)

DOB: (redacted)

DATE OF ADMISSION: 9/13/2022

AGE: 37

ATTENDING PHYSICIAN: Lenora Lynn, MD

CONSULTING PHYSICIAN: Ephraim Kandi, MD, PhD

CONSULTATION DATE: 09/13/2022

ADMITTING DIAGNOSES: **Acute Psychosis, NOS r/o toxicity**
Right temporal lobe lesion, favors
malignancy
Secondary Meningitis
Secondary Encephalitis
Failure to thrive

REASON FOR CONSULTATION: **Primary neoplastic lesion of the brain**
Secondary CNS inflammatory change
Secondary CNS infectious process
Emergency radiotherapy evaluation
Characterization of neoplasm

HISTORY OF PRESENT ILLNESS:

Ms. (redacted) is a 37-year-old female who was brought in by local
law enforcement after relatives requested a welfare check on the
patient and her mother. She had reportedly barricaded herself
within her home, and was escalatingly hostile and violent on initial
encounter with the responding officer, who noted that the patient
appeared disheveled and neglected. She was inappropriately fearful
of the officer and the officer noticed evidence of violence on her
person. Emergency medical services were requested, and the patient
was forcibly restrained, sedated, and transported to the Emergency
Department where her behavior prompted involuntary Psychiatric
confinement. She was found to be dehydrated and visibly
malnourished, and IV hydration was initiated, and she was placed on
telemetry and pulse oximetry monitoring. Emergency Psychiatric

evaluation was undertaken, and Neurology was consulted for findings of decreased mental status and disorganized thinking. Gross peripheral neurological examination at that time was non-focal. Toxicity panel was negative. CT scan revealed a 12 cm obliterating right temporal lobe lesion with associated intraparenchymal hemorrhage and parenchymal swelling and evidence of meningeal inflammation, but surprisingly little to no herniation. Appearance of the tumor suggests malignancy. The patient was admitted to the ICU, intubated, sedated, and intracranial monitoring was initiated. Opening pressure was 22, and efforts were initiated by protocol to decrease intracranial pressure.

Neurosurgery received a stat consultation request to evaluate the patient for emergent radiotherapy and tissue characterization biopsy. Psychiatric evaluation initiated and then suspended to allow for urgent interventions. Internal Medicine evaluation for stabilization and medical clearance is ongoing.

PAST MEDICAL HISTORY: Recent outpatient evaluation nine months prior for headache, recurrent nosebleeds. Patient advised by primary physician to complete workup, but had apparently not scheduled elective imaging. History of any carcinogenic exposures is unknown.

PAST SURGICAL HISTORY: Unremarkable.

MEDICATIONS: Patient took a daily multivitamin prior to admission.

ALLERGIES: NKDA

SOCIAL HISTORY: Per maternal aunt, patient was a never smoker, rare alcohol, no history of illicits.   Graduate education, worked as an astrophysicist and college professor. Married, no children.

PHYSICAL EXAMINATION:

Neurological examination: deferred, patient currently sedated, paralyzed, intubated. Exam done in Emergency Department reviewed.

Head and Neck: Patient is normocephalic, intraventricular monitor in place left side, atraumatic appearance. Neck grossly normal, but there is slight distension of the neck veins. Protuberant tympanic membranes, right greater than left. Mucous membranes moist, dentition normal, halitotic. Poor recent dental hygiene.

Chest: Lungs clear to auscultation with basilar crackles likely related to hyperinflation, intubation.

Heart: S1S2 normal without murmur, rub, gallop. PMI as expected.

Breast/Genitalia exam: Deferred. Grossly normal external appearance.

Abdomen: Soft. Unremarkable. No evidence of organomegaly. No masses.

Extremities: Grossly normal in appearance. No integumentary lesions. Hands are grossly soiled and there is dark material embedded under the fingernails.

IMAGING: Pertinent findings as noted in the HPI. MRI Pending.

IMPRESSION: Right temporal lobe tumor of indeterminate cellular origin with associated intracranial hemorrhage, resulting in significantly elevated intracranial pressure, psychosis secondary to mass effect, threat of herniation secondary to mass effect, secondary meningitis, secondary encephalitis.

PLAN:

Patient will be taken to MRI under anesthesia monitoring for further imaging. Will plan to initiate steroid protocol and immediate radiotherapy to control intracranial pressure and try to prevent herniation. Further treatment plans will be dictated by patient's medical fitness and response to therapy. Tissue biopsy will be deferred until patient is medically stable and if treatment outcomes suggest tissue characterization is warranted. Prognosis is grim. Further recommendations to follow based on results of imaging and response to radiation therapy...

...and additional human remains were discovered on the subject's property.

The first victim, a male, was found in the plastic storage bin beneath the exterior deck. Cause of death was penetrating trauma from a crossbow injury with exsanguination. He was later identified as the landscaper, (redacted), age 42.

The second, another male, was found in the downstairs chest freezer, the victim of repeated blunt trauma. His injuries were consistent with repeated blows from the baseball bat recovered from the umbrella stand near the front door. Blood and hair recovered from the bat matched the victim. He was positively identified as the subject's husband, Jamie (redacted), age 40.

The final victim was stuffed into the cabinets beneath the large central island in the kitchen. Cause of death was repeated penetrating trauma. A hunting knife recovered from the subject's music room had physical evidence, blood and tissue, that matched the third victim. She was identified as the subject's mother, Marjorie (redacted), age 62...

Anillo de Sangre

At convent school, I was the enforcer of the secret laws.

If two could not agree to an appropriate compromise, the question was solved pragmatically. After dark, outside the high stone walls, the Circle drawn in chalk on the ground. A layer of magic for adolescent *brujas*. A scarf to bind one wrist of each girl to the other; by whatever means were necessary, one would be forced out of the Circle, out of its protection. She the loser, forced to acquiesce without further argument to the victor.

By the time I was ten years old, not even the older girls dared test my will. My desires were complied with thereafter; a trip to the Circle with me always resulted in a loss of flesh.

The law of the Circle a secret, just as were the decisions it upheld. Thus was created an uneasy peace in a hornet's nest of *Latinas*…

But other girls were not the biggest problem I faced.

The Devil was.

It came to us unannounced. Insidiously disguised. An old evil, following fast on the heels of a visit from Death.

Sister Cortesía, *La Superiora*, neither young nor old, hung herself, unexpectedly, explicitly, using her own rosary. One end onto the coat hook behind her door and then she had found enough will to simply slump to the floor, allowing her weight to tighten the iridescent beads around her throat so cruelly that *La Virgen* was embedded in her skin.

I needed to keep the Circle intact.

Perhaps there the Devil couldn't reach me.

But the Devil knows fear, reads thoughts. Makes a place for the sinner – not to hide, rather to come forward in the world. Not having to follow all the rules set down – particularly, if you believed the legends – in stone.

Those rules a prison of sorts. Those who could have protected me locked inside that prison. And if you are locked inside, trapped, the enemy always knows where to find you.

Worse yet, there is no escape. The Devil had reached in and touched Sister Cortesía. We were none of us safe.

That suicide, that sin, opened the doors to even greater evil. The premonition in my bones when it started, and I saw the willful blindness of those who should have seen. Girls disappearing, while none of our holy adults made protest.

I awoke to the noises, heard the furtive industry beside my bed. A shadow, creeping there. Slurping the water from the cup on the nightstand under the window, bathing in the moonlight.

I could only close my eyes tight against the darkness of the room, feigning sleep, pretending. The cold finger against my ribs, reminding me what waited on the other side of my fright.

It knew I was awake. After Sister Cortesía, I refused to wear the cross around my neck. I slept with a sliver of broken chalk in my hand, ready to run.

My conscience afire, twelve nights to hide in plain sight, and on the thirteenth, the moon, my guilt, the cleansing rain —who could say? Something needed doing.

Those sounds, I could bear it no longer. I stood in the dim dark of the ward, climbed atop my bed for all to see and hear and made my bargain with the Devil.

"Meet *me* in the Circle, and no more." Resolute, these words for the Evil that walked among us. Determined despite the scared relief in the eyes of the other girls. Moonglow lit the moisture of their tears, made mirrors of their sleepless eyes as I drew the Monster's gaze.

My fingers curled. Around chalk in one pocket. Curled around a rosary in the other. Leading the way to the gate. Like the rider on the pale horse. Hell following after, ever after.

"Outside *my* Circle, by *my* rules, by my hand, and you have no further grievance or claim upon me and mine," I said. "No retaliation against one outside the Circle, for it governs only what exists between the two of us." To these rules the Devil bound, by mere words a promise extracted. The words of a child who had not known defeat.

A beloved bargain for the Demon. Poor keeper of promises. Not acquainted with truth. I knew why it had come. Searching for me. Wanting me more than its own deceit.

Not even the nuns knew the secret of my blood. I could
no better be held to an oath than the Beast. *La sangre
inmunda.* In the chaos following my orphaning, they had
forgotten to baptize me.

I removed my sweater to attend the wet pavement.
Friction and water melting chalk into nothingness. The
Circle created, smeared into being. Aglow under the
moon, under the mulberry tree that reached skeletal
fingers over the cloister walls as if to accuse, as if to snatch
away.

It can be anything, anyone. This time it chose to be a
tiny, pretty thing. Stepping forward from nothingness. A
face from an old picture, slipped into the back of my
Bible long ago, the edges furred. The one I dreamed of,
would search for, and never find. I forgot my plan in the
ashes of that dream, that I could have the one thing I
truly wanted.

Then anger. I could ill afford sentimentality when I was
here to pay for souls. Then the Devil nodded to me,
somber, a flash of something behind the eyes, a reminder.
A *Catrina.* Death's head soft, like the moth. Like a
mother. Her death on my hands, for she could not
survive the insult of my birth.

El Satan, wearing her skin. To bear witness, it told me,
because,

"it is flesh

which is the currency here
flesh must be paid"

The slipping sibilant voice slid from those lips, not unlike my own. It grated and scratched like dry leaves scattering on the pavement in the autumn wind.

"my soul is belief
here there are rules
of existence
and in the circle you are flesh and blood"

"Join me within; the Circle shall judge, for it is Alpha, it is Omega, *Amen."* I whispered my words into the wind. She caught up my hand, and we entered together.

Twelve crimson drops, one for each night it had come, for each girl it had taken, for each year of my life. These I offered, these it accepted. A bride-price. The sharp end of a rosary cross pressed deep into my little finger. All to make a crimson fairy ring around a promised bower.

Me within.

Death without, trapped yet in that sacred space. Between blood and chalk I trapped the Devil on that lonely night. By my bargain outside *my* circle.

Banished from that place forever. Its screams to haunt my dreams alone.

Or are they mine I hear?

The dream is always the same. Never about the crash, which is probably what confounds the psychologists.

The dream is about **him**. A nondescript man, graying hair, neither too old nor too young. His eyes are kind, and compelling.   His flannel shirt looks worn and soft. He is speaking but I cannot hear what he says.

No impatience when I don't respond. Strong hands grab the front of my harness to drag me through the grass, away from the spiraling smoke that curls urgently into a perfect blue sky. That autumn morning sky, the kind you wish you could reproduce, a day on which you should sit outside a café down on Earth, sipping coffee and enjoying an apple donut before you wander through the farmer's market. Perhaps feeling that first bite of cool weather but refusing to return to the car for your sweatshirt, knowing the sun will warm you soon enough.

He goes back for something, it seems, moves out of my field of vision. And then the explosion, which would have finished me had I not been moved to safety.

The psychologists find it all very interesting. I understand why it confounds them, but I struggle less to assign much meaning to it. The flight investigation revealed that no civilians lived within 50 miles of the crash site, no human remains were identified or recovered. Drag marks on the ground and broken grass clumps showed that I pulled myself to safety despite injuries that left me paralyzed from the waist down.

The flight recordings do reveal that Sagittarius was still functioning, analyzing the conditions of the crash in real time. Sagittarius was advising me to clear the site due to the danger of combustion and explosion, reading my proximity sensors.

I have listened to that machine voice over and over, almost an exhortation, "Commander Vega, evacuate combustion zone immediately..." but I do not remember my droid speaking to me at all.

I understand their assessment; it seems clear that I have conflated Sagittarius with a human caregiver, perhaps in my pain and disorientation after the crash I conjured a father figure to comfort my psyche.

I simply nod and acknowledge that they could be right, but I consider it much ado about nothing. The identity or even the reality of this phantom, this imago, does not distress me in the least. And the dream is far from traumatic, if anything, having that as my only memory of the worst day of my life is comforting.

It is probably the reason I was cleared so quickly to return to piloting test flights at all.

1

Fisher Vega faced the curious reporters with a wary amusement. She expected their questions to have less to do with the mission and more to do with the tabloid-worthy developments surrounding International Space Command's assignment of the four pilots to this new deep space mission.

"You're taking *Sagittarius*, the prototype that caused the crash which injured you, and your husband is-" The question, as expected, was loaded.

"My *ex-husband*," Fisher reminded them with a wry smile, keeping her tone both gentle and neutral.

"Yes. Commander Springer is at the helm of the *Winter*, and the most advanced of your droids is Aries."

"The *Winter*'s mission goes furthest into deep space. Its directives hold the greatest risk. Besides, he's going to need the most advanced AI my technology can provide. Commander Springer is, shall we say, somewhat technologically challenged."

"In what way is he challenged by technology?" asked one of the reporters, in a slightly defensive tone that suggested she might be one of his starry-eyed groupies.

"He repels it," Fisher replied, hoping there would be better questions than this one, knowing that it was unlikely. She was gratified when the group laughed, but she didn't feel particularly good about slighting a peer commander on the mission. Oh well. He'd get his chance to retaliate later. At this very press conference, should he so choose.

"Doesn't it bother you that Sagittarius' failure was the cause of your test-flight crash ten years ago?" Another reporter, this one a friend, and Fisher smiled, because this was the meat of what she wanted the tax-paying public to understand.

"Sagittarius was just a baby then. You've got to walk before you can run, right? There's a reason we call it a test flight."

"But that failure-" someone else tried to break in, but Fisher held up a hand, signaling for patience.

"Listen, it was not technically the droid's failure. It was mine. AI failures are ultimately *human* failures. Sagittarius and I have learned quite a bit from those early flights, and he will fly again on the *Autumn* as part of my android crew."

"*He?*" The friend again, with a bit of humor in the question. Justified, as Fisher had just gender-specified a robotic pilot. The human anthropomorphizing her creation.

"Well, my horoscope today told me not to pass on a sexy Sagittarius," Fisher quipped. "I'm taking that as a very lucky sign that my droid assignments are appropriate. Thanks for your time."

She left the podium to laughter and applause, yielding to the next victim, taking her place in the lineup at the back of the stage with the three other astronauts slated to command the remaining crafts. She was careful to avoid standing next to Brian, her ex.

Fisher's eyes were inexorably drawn to the VIP section of the auditorium; it was packed with those dignitaries and family members of the mission crew who were invited to pad the crowd with allies of ISC's agenda. Every space agency director since time immemorial wanted everyday citizens to see the commanders as human sacrificial lambs, individuals who were loved, who would be missed, just like in any other family.

But hers was not any other family. Fisher's mother had agreed to relocation to the Mars colony to allow for the possibility she could see her daughters, one who was a deep-space pilot, and the other who was now married to one. And perhaps a son-in-law whom she had always been fond of despite the rift he had created in the family.

Fisher located Hannah immediately and watched her for several moments. Hannah was a pro at avoiding eye contact with Fisher, a pro at avoiding any contact, which was probably for the best.

When they were very young, barely out of the nursery, Hannah was the kind of sister who, if she liked the color of Fisher's ball better than the color of the one she had received, would pirate the one she desired. Making off with it and claiming it by being seen everywhere with it, until the grownups could no longer recall that it wasn't actually hers. She did the same thing with clothing, jewelry, and shampoo as she and Fisher got older.

Fisher let Hannah have these small tyrannies, because she had not cared for specific things in the way that Hannah had, and was generally avoidant of conflict.

So Hannah, in her way, had groomed Fisher into sisterly compliance, or perhaps Fisher had indulged Hannah overmuch. By the time Hannah decided she wanted Fisher's husband, it was far too late to correct her behavior.

He was an FLK. It means funny-looking kid, one of the first dehumanizing acronyms you learn in medical school. Pediatrics. Somehow the term survived all the language softening and sensitivity training of the 21st century. It is inappropriate as hell, but you never forget the logic. If you see an FLK, first you look at the parents. If they are FLKs as well, the kid is probably all right. If not, the kid likely has some sort of syndrome.

The first time I met Brian was with a group of friends out at a bar. He was an FLK that had grown into an FLA. Appealing but rather odd face that was nonetheless open and apparently joyful. I'm trying to avoid the word ugly here, even though it was used often to refer to him. I'm sure he knew it. You don't grow up with a face like that and remain unaware of the talk. There was a bit of mischief in those eyes. He was an Emergency Medicine resident, a year or two ahead of me. I was in Surgery, probably my second year. The Surgery residents were not completely unwinding, as our drinking was eating into the very little sleep we ever got. The EM crew were well-rested and a bit rowdier, settled in for a long night of revelry.

His ears were not necessarily enormous, but they stuck out from his head like jug handles, giving him a mouselike appearance; you know, the one with the red knickers that I won't name because some still ridiculously huge conglomerate leisure corporation might charge me for it.

I stayed on the periphery of the group, thinking about robotics, as usual, not needing to be the center of *attention, content as always to listen to the others. I learned that night that Brian was smart, hilarious, and kind. Apparently his looks had made him empathic to the other sufferers in the world.*

And a high-achiever. One of the other women in our group mentioned that he had been a pilot. Maybe still was. Our training program was large, at the intersection of the military and civilian worlds. About half the residents in any given specialty were still enlisted. Brian was one of them. The program sent a lot of candidates to the space command. Pilot doctors are the specialty.

2

Fisher sat up night after night, running fuel consumption algorithms for a number of scenarios, syncing protocols among the four starships. All of the Deep Space Exploration Vehicles (DSEVs) for the upcoming mission were integrated with droid technology that she had developed during her post-doctoral work.

Sadly, the twelve mission droids were of varying age and operating systems. They had been outfitted with the same upgrades to allow them to function in synchrony, and each was programmed with variable learning software that would enable them to adapt for their individual areas of expertise. Each droid had the capability to 'crosstrain' the other AI entities on their mission craft, a workaround nod to the possibility of inflight failures or malfunctions. She also had them interface with the droids on the other DSEVs to create a sort of communal understanding of the different challenges each would encounter.

Finally, she had equipped them to build new responses to old problems based on what Fisher deemed experiential outcome analysis. It was the equivalent of learning from mistakes made by other missions, individuals, artificial intelligence failures, and other factors that might create scenarios where a desirable outcome could not be achieved.

Details about each commander's sleep patterns, hygiene, diet, stress response, and mood could be factored into this analysis, as well as anything that could adversely affect external performance, such as communication shortcomings.

As soon as Sagittarius was upgraded, it began making significant and intrusive predictions about how and what Fisher's diet, stress level, and mood were likely to affect any given mission trajectory. The other commanders were subject to the same analysis from their respective control droids, and this made Fisher slightly more unpopular than she already was, if that were possible.

My second encounter with Brian was in Emergency Services. I was with a more senior resident, dealing with the aftermath of a starship loader malfunction. Apparently, my senior and Brian knew one another, and she stopped to speak with him but failed to introduce me. I could have cared less, having orders and other tasks to prepare for our patient.

Later, as I was working alone at a console, Brian found an excuse to wander over and speak to me.

"Didn't I see you at the canteen the other night?" he asked, but it wasn't too terrible an opening; I could see he wasn't dropping a line on me. He held out his hand and introduced himself.

I only smiled distractedly and replied, "I'm nobody special."

He laughed. "Are you sure you're a surgeon? I mean, you have a down-to-earth perspective that I don't generally ascribe to your group."

I'd never been complimented in such a way before. My mild-mannered, slightly odd, self-deprecating personality tended to make me more of a target. I did better with computers and machines than people. That was a conscious choice. I noticed his expression remained somewhat quizzical, but I didn't offer my name. It was public knowledge, and I was serious in my assessment that it wasn't important. I suspected he already knew it, but I was wrong.

Several months later, I inadvertently misplaced my operator's license in one of the military rovers, traveling from a bar to a party with others on another forced social outing. I didn't even realize it had been misplaced, and Brian had found it.

Apparently, when he had inquired with other colleagues how best to return it, he had caused a bit of a stir. They teased him mercilessly; the implication being that we must have hooked up, and in the chaos of shedding and donning our clothing, I had left the license behind. The general consensus was that I must have been pretty impaired to find him attractive enough for such an assignation, in the load bed of a rover, no less.

When I heard the rumor, I was furious that anyone would assume that he couldn't attract a girlfriend because of the way he looked. So when he returned the license I made sure there was an audience to see me whispering in his ear, only my thanks, but of course none of them knew that was all it was. He obliged me by turning a bright raspberry color, poor man.

That's how it all started; he saw that I had no problem with the idea of us together. His embarrassment confirmed his attraction. And not so eventually we did what they had accused us of in the first place, because if I were supposed to have committed the crime I figured I might as well actually have the fun.

What other people thought meant fuck-all to me.

The DSEVs were transported to space dock forty-five days in advance of launch, to be retrofitted with the cobalt decay drives that provided primary power for the starships.

The shielded reactors powered flight capability, and the nickel remainder was harvested to support the electrical core. Each drive provided self-sustaining, renewable propulsion and energy. Space thermodynamics negated nearly every concern about overheating.

Fisher took a shuttle to space dock thirty days before launch and took over the flight operations prep. Despite the urging of colleagues and Command, she remained with her ship, disembarking only to take rations in the mess. She reviewed algorithms for the droid assignments, ensuring that they were synchronized among the four vehicles.

Each starship had a command droid responsible for systems and life support, and this droid was also equipped with flight protocols. A second droid was assigned a scientific algorithm, and functioned as a medical/biosystem/biosuspension analyst. The third droid had an engineering function, and monitored fuel and mechanical systems and materiel.

Solo missions required no quarantine, and the other commanders were not slated to arrive until 96 hours prior to launch. But Brian arrived early, about a week after she did, and Fisher was only made aware of this detail when he paid her an unexpected visit on the *Autumn.*

She was ensuring that there was adequate redundancy among the droids to consider them able to cross-reference the data needed to perform all possible tasks. The algorithm looked for any and all potential failures and posited solutions that any of the AI could reference in order to avoid mission critical interruptions in function due to unanticipated error. She was brought out of a concentrated reverie by Sagittarius' voice.

"Greetings, Commander Springer."

It took Fisher several moments to process what she had just heard, and by the time the name trickled down into her consciousness, Brian had come up behind her. He still used the same soap he always had, so it could be no one else. Fisher did not like the fact that his scent had the same disarming effect on her that it always had.

Without taking her attention off her console, she said calmly, "Sagittarius, go actual."

A nearby bulkhead seemed to briefly reshape itself, and the eight-foot android stepped out, its position located it between the two humans. Its titanium body was both intimidating and familiar, the result of focus group study that determined the best possible appearance should both provide a sense of security and have a humanoid relatability. It was felt that this would increase the ease with which human operators would accept assignments involving droids.

Fisher made their exoskeletons bicolored, with two tone metallic skins. She was a bit of a comic-book nerd, and her decision recalled Tony Stark's idea to make the Iron Man more relatable by painting the metal like a performance sportscar. Then she took the project a step further and gave them bodies either masculinized or feminized out of a sense of fairness and need for representation.

The focus groups had loved it; humans responded best to their reflected body imagery. The droids themselves had been featured in recruiting adverts for Space Command and were minor celebrities in their own right.

Fisher was fairly certain that the average citizen could not pick her out of a line-up, but nearly everyone recognized Sagittarius' blue metallic image. But he had gotten an upgrade that she knew no one had expected; she'd adjusted the exos, made them inhumanly oversized, based on calculations about optimal utility for mechanical function, wingspan, and reach.

Springer took a step back, and Fisher was gratified. She knew it was petty, but so be it.

"Commander Springer." She felt as though she had to bite off those words one by one, and she still did so with difficulty.

She did not favor him by turning her attention from her work or asking what he needed. Several awkward moments passed in silence. Sagittarius was inhumanly still, positioned between them like a large floor lamp or a tree.

"I hope you are well." Fisher was surprised that one so facile at making small talk failed at it miserably in her company. It was a sad measure of what had been lost. He continued, stammering on, unnecessarily and awkwardly excruciating, "…your sister sends her love."

"Deception detected, Commander Springer," Sagittarius interjected.   Fisher smiled.

"You turned your prize android into a goddamned lie-detector?!" Brian went from zero to frustration very quickly. It had been a hallmark of the latter stages of their marriage. Fisher turned to look at him, and was unsurprised to see how red his neck and ears already were. She wondered if he had the good grace to be embarrassed. She still couldn't tell.

"Are you suggesting you don't understand why I would need one? Perhaps I should have thought to make that upgrade sooner and saved us all a lot of trouble," Fisher mused calmly.

"Maximilian told me that the mission protocol doesn't just call for a command droid on each one of the starships, but that you made Sagittarius the Mission Command Droid, that-" Brian gestured in disgust at the metal monolith standing next to them. "-this *thing* can override protocols on the *Winter*, can override decisions made by my droids, made by *me*, for that matter. That it can second-guess mission objectives in real time."

"Is there a point to this visit, Commander?" Fisher managed to sound bored, a minor triumph in her general inability to deal with him with any equanimity.

"I think I deserve to know why external command controls are built into the mission." Brian crossed his arms, not realizing it was a common tell that Fisher had learned meant he was insecure in his position, that he felt threatened. Others read it differently, and she knew it was rare when he acted this sternly that he did not get his way.

"Sagittarius has the longest learning algorithm history, the closest thing to experiential knowledge that any AI entity will obtain. He used this knowledge to build the other droids, and can use it to teach them. He will function as a background reference in their programming. Besides, redundancy will equate to additional safeguards-"

"Christ! You refer to it as a 'he?!'"

"As a matter of inclusivity. He is part of my crew, and has been an extremely useful adjunct to my human skillset throughout his deployment. Even in the earliest days he made protocol adjustments that benefitted my mission directives."

"He couldn't save your legs," Brian observed calmly. It stung. A lot. Although Fisher did find it gratifying that while mocking her for anthropomorphizing her creation, he was also responding as though Sagittarius were a secondary male rival. They could both hit below the belt.

"And *you* couldn't save your marriage," she replied, turning back to her computer.

"I never meant for…what happened… to happen. It started before we could make sense of it, and then-" he trailed off, his defenses ineffectual as ever. Just like that, she was murderously angry again.

"Make sense of it? In what way? It would have been bad enough if you had found some stranger, but infinitely more understandable. But in this case, the other woman definitely knew you were married, since she was standing only one person removed from you at your wedding."

Fisher hated to talk about it, but if presented with the opportunity it was frightening how easy it was for her to find ways to wound him verbally. Hannah was smart; by avoiding Fisher she remained out of range of this kind of ordinance.

"And what about ISIS?" Brian was quieter now, which allowed her to hear his pain.

"That again? Was I supposed to rewrite history because I had met you? Because you proposed?"

"You were supposed to disclose!"

Here, Sagittarius interjected once more, logically misunderstanding. "Does Commander Springer not understand the lack of utility of his ISIS objection?"

"No, Sagittarius, his objection is personal." Fisher sighed. This was not an optimal time for Sagittarius to 'learn.'

"I do not understand." Sagittarius fell silent, expecting an explanation. Fisher noted Brian's panicked expression, and capitulated.

"Sagittarius, go virtual." As quickly as he had emerged, Sagittarius was subsumed into the bulkhead and the two commanders were left physically alone in the small space, their anger deflated.

Fisher had no desire to address Brian's thwarted expectations about procreation; apparently once that dream had attached to her, without any inquiry as to whether the dream was shared. He had, apparently, transferred those hopes to Hannah, but the two of them had been together more than fifteen years, and remained childless. Fisher wondered whether Brian believed it a punishment for his infidelity. She suspected he did. He was superstitious that way.

As if reading her mind, he turned away, and with a single backward glance, left her alone again, with her algorithms, and her droids, the only children she would ever have.

Pilot doctors.

Ideal for deep space solo missions. If one can perform all manner of interventions in situations of illness to others, theoretically, they can be performed for oneself.

In theory. The psychologists felt it was second nature to perform non-invasive healthcare, but wondered how highly trained individuals would perform in situations where surgical intervention was needed. Overcoming the burden of self-harm, the infliction of necessary pain, and the limitations of intellectual and physical function in the face of extremis were significant obstacles to developing a training program.

Necessity drove it as much as willing volunteers.

Deep space commanders were enrolled, and using a combination of mental exercise, relaxation techniques, and cutting-edge technology, ISIS was developed to train an individual in self-surgery.

Many thought the program name was an acronym, but not so. Isis was the wife of the god Osiris, who was dismembered by his brother, Set. Isis collected the parts of Osiris' body and brought them together, surgically reconstructing and resurrecting him. Some versions of the story suggest she recovered every part but one – his missing manhood was never found; a technicality that would hardly keep a god from being posthumously able to father another immortal, Horus.

I was a willing volunteer from the latter stages of my medical education. By the time my residency started I had already removed my own appendix. Pragmatically, knowing my planned career trajectory, I volunteered for a second go, and during my internship successfully auto-excised my gallbladder.

My aptitude for these tasks was studied in order to determine how best to train others to undertake such endeavors. I volunteered to staff the lab and use my AI advances to analyze the data.

One night, several months before I met Brian, I was alone, working late on improving support protocols for the droids, when I realized there was another intervention I could make.

It would require no new incision, the appendiceal removal access could be used, and using the pelvic camera and two staple loads, I could accomplish self-sterilization in under 15 minutes.

"Dr. Vega, you are diverging from investigational protocol. Control monitoring by outside personnel is part of the study algorithm. IRB insistence on failsafes during trials must be restated." Sagittarius, ever the voice of my conscience, did not fail to question my motives.

"These are the best conditions to mimic mission environment, where there are no failsafes or control maneuvers. Under those conditions, I would have only a droid, identical to your programming, correct? And my own skill in the face of considerable distress."

"Your observation regarding conditions is correct; however, deception is detected generally in your answer,"

Sagittarius replied. "I cannot log that as a justification to break protocol."

"Then log that it is nobody's business," I said.

"Sterilization protocol calls for-" Sagittarius attempted to run interference, but I cut him off.

"Override protocol." My order had supremacy over his programming.

"Then I must advise you that your current course is unwise," was the rejoinder. "The pre-sterilization counseling is a prerequisite-"

I interrupted him, and at the same time began my breathing exercises and anesthetic injection at the surgical site, flooding the skin and deeper tissues. I paused when I felt the jolt of the needle tip contact the exquisitely innervated peritoneum and took my time ensuring I deposited enough medication to numb it.

"Sagittarius, begin learning algorithm. Is the protocol identical for males and females?" I asked, determined that my droid should benefit from my own anomalous behavior. Droids needed to be exposed to many human diversions from expectation if they were to maximize their ability to 'understand' unpredictability in modeling of behavior.

"Dr. Vega, you know the answer to that question."

"Humor me, Sagittarius."

"I don't understand the request as stated." Sagittarius gave his usual response to my use of vernacular.

"Answer my initial question." My tone betrayed my frustration.

"It is not."

"Why not?" I asked, entirely curious about the answer. Androids have no true ability to conjecture.

"My evaluation of the available data suggest a social-emotional cause rooted in principles of paternalism," Sagittarius replied. I smiled.

"And what role does paternalism have in determining two differing protocols, Sagittarius?"

"There is an apparent protective interest toward propagation and maintenance of the species."

"Are the contributions of either sex less or more critical to species survival?" I asked.

"It would appear they are equally important." Sagittarius' answer sounded more deferent than it was.

"Are humans an endangered species?" I followed up my initial inquiry, leading my droid's evaluation and unpacking the logic required for it to learn my motivation.

"They are not," Sagittarius quickly concluded.

"Do those who are eligible for the ISIS protocols represent a critical number of the affected species?"

"No. They represent a superminority."

"What is the calculated percentage of existing inability to procreate among those eligible for ISIS?" I asked.

"For all possible etiologies, including self-election, based on all available data from human studies, the calculated percentage is 4.82753. I do not have a reliable error rate, and the sampled data may poorly represent the subset of humans affected by ISIS."

"If you like, you can adjust for two variables for which you should have behavioral data within the Space Command and military databases," I explained. "Space Command personnel may have higher rates of self-election as it pertains to their overall fitness for deep space solo missions, while military personnel may indeed have lower rates."

"This dichotomy is not logical," Sagittarius observed.

"No. But it makes sense when you learn that historically, military personnel are rewarded financially for having children; their pay increases as a direct result of the birth of each child," I pointed out.

"Reevaluating data. The additional information results in a new calculated percentage of 5.33741." It only took Sagittarius five seconds to recalculate.

"And would the theoretical sterilization of every human eligible for ISIS threaten the viability of the species?" I asked.

"It would not."

"Can you now explain the utility of using different protocols in counseling by gender?"

"No. The protocol lacks valid utility and is inexplicable."

"Sagittarius, supply the definition for the word 'discrimination,' and contextualize it within the parameters of applying unidentical counseling requirements…" I concluded, already aware that our conversation was interfering with the efficacy of my anesthetic dose. I'd let too much time elapse, and the effects were wearing off.

"Stress hormone levels are spiking," Sagittarius noted unnecessarily as I proceeded to make my incision. I held pressure on the wound and administered a shot of epinephrine to assist me in keeping focus. It hit me like a freight train, and I took a deep breath and plunged into an act of rebellion disguised as self-determination. It was something I couldn't teach a droid to understand.

In hindsight, when I lost my legs, I felt even more justified. Pseudo-clairvoyant. Deception detected. Self-deception.

4

Four days prior to launch, Sagittarius revisited Fisher's conversation with Brian. It surprised her; although she had taught the droid to resolve any anomalies or deficiencies in its understanding, she could not understand in the moment why their exchange had been prioritized.

"I do not understand the conclusion of your exchange with Commander Springer regarding ISIS." Sagittarius could not know how human-like this random interjection seemed, although he was beginning to collect and understand examples of non sequitur. "You said, '*his objection was personal,*' yet Commander Springer did not undergo sterilization."

"Commander Springer was selfishly concerned about the propagation of his own DNA. So he traded me in," Fisher replied, without a hint of irony. She understood that AI interpretation of the word selfish carried no derogatory connotation without further negative context, so she meant the droid to decipher it as an observation of human self-interest.

"Traded you in?" Sagittarius was asking for clarification, but Fisher hesitated to explain, so he continued, uncannily quickly, "Your sister can provide the necessary material?"

It was slightly disturbing to hear it put in such a way, but fundamentally Sagittarius was not wrong.

"Yes. But they seem to have failed." Fisher was surprised at her own guilt about this. She was more certain about how it affected Brian than her sister.

"Your spouse has some faulty code?" This time Aries was asking, using intervessel communication from her physical location on the *Winter*. It was an abject reminder to Fisher that all twelve of the droids were listening, and learning, in real time. It should have disturbed her, but didn't.

"Please recharacterize Commander Springer as my colleague as he is no longer a 'spouse,'" Fisher requested this so that she could avoid hearing further mischaracterization of their relationship. The blinking indicator on her heads-up display reminded her that Aries was waiting for an answer.

"That's certainly one way to put it," she replied, not sure what was more amusing, the fact that she was discussing her failed marriage with a machine or its apt characterization of the situation. "But I suppose all humans have faulty code. It's a frailty of the species. And the reason why I like to keep at least six planets between myself and Commander Springer whenever possible."

How do you forgive yourself? For not being enough.

For not being the boy your father wanted, the daughter your mother needed, the wife your husband could not live without, the sister your sister would respect.

For not being the pilot you could have been, or the engineer the world needed.

I can only overcome these failings by making sure that my legacy improves as many strangers' lives as possible, since history has shown that my actions are hopelessly inadequate to be of any use to those closest to me.

5

Deep into the launch protocol, Sagittarius noted an anomaly.

"Commander, Aries is running a new algorithm subset," he said.

"Identify subject and expand for evaluation." Fisher responded automatically.   She confirmed steep parabolic mission trajectories for the four ships, launch was synchronized, and critical countdown had begun. The trajectories looked most like the embedded curves of a chambered Nautilus; the shortest curve for the *Spring,* the longest belonging to the *Winter.*

"I am unable to fully characterize it, as it appears she has adopted particular encryption parameters to obscure its objectives." Sagittarius responded. "As I cannot assess the likelihood that this is not a system glitch and may represent a critical failure, I must recommend we abort launch."

"Evaluate signature patterning and report," Fisher requested, without any indication that the recommendation should be undertaken.

"It appears to be an acquisitive pattern. Perhaps a reasoned learning protocol, problem-solving, or predictive analytics," Sagittarius told her.

"Percentage of similar activity among all droids collectively?" Fisher inquired.

"Forty-seven percent. Similar patterns running in nine of twelve droids."

"It falls within expected response to launch and mission initiation responsibilities?" Fisher prompted.

"Preliminary assessment would suggest so," Sagittarius allowed.

"Monitor for change, continue evaluation and decryption as background to launch responsibilities, and report findings.   Request to abort mission commencement denied." With this, Fisher returned her attention to a successful launch.

"Instructions confirmed, Commander. Launch sequence timing synchronized. Mission clock starting in T minus seven minutes. Docking reversal initiated. Cobalt drives upgraded from standby to idle." Sagittarius resumed his comforting patter as he reported the stages of countdown, and Fisher largely forgot about the anomaly.

She would have cause to regret her human failure in retrospect.

I should have recognized Aries' advanced capability to wrestle mission control from Sagittarius.

My simple, deprecating response to her question about Brian's 'faulty code', coupled with my remarks at the press conference had only been fodder for a suggestible and highly advanced learning algorithm. Aries had concluded that Commander Springer's technological shortcomings and 'miscoding' threatened the Winter's mission. That such a failure was critical, necessitating lethal measures to correct it, a solution so absolute only a machine could support it.

By the time Sagittarius unraveled this encrypted deception, the Winter was beyond its safe-return boundary. Indeed, all four starships were irrevocably committed to interstellar flight.

Only the Autumn carried enough fuel reserves to intercept them, and even then, it was unclear whether I would be able to save Brian, and if so, whether either of us would ever make it home.

To be continued…

Discovery

Tokyo, Kyobashi District, 2012

Pink umbrella. It bobs along below him in a sea of black ones during a busy rush-hour, central-Tokyo commute as he surveys the sidewalk from the second floor of his converted warehouse loft.

It is probably technically a parasol, wooden supports, hand-painted linen, cherry blossoms. Some kind of heirloom belonging to a geisha-wannabe, boy-band-loving rich girl, he thinks. Daddy brought it back from Thailand, and she carries it because no one else has one. Entirely impractical for the weather. Cute.

Roku has no use for cute.

He sees it again in the rack, drying alongside others in the entryway at *Belle's.* He never understood the premise of the name. Western. The restaurant is some sort of casual Asian fusion. Upscale. A bistro with a nice bar. He decides such an item must belong to the hostess.

She sets out a sandwich board with the specials on the sidewalk just as he is walking by, her outfit timeless and fashionable. It is just this side of summer, still cool in the afternoons, and she has paired her short sleeved black turtleneck with cropped black tights and ballet slippers. Her black hair twisted up behind her head, casual-appearing but he knows she took her time with it. Something that reminds him of a black and white movie he watched once, with subtitles, Audrey Hepburn in that same ensemble. Parisian, smart. It suits her, and she knows it. Bright, big eyes, lashes long as a doe's.

She is built like a dancer, slim and spare. She moves like a dancer. He notices, and suspects everyone else does as well. She notes his presence and his attention. Her mouth curls up at the corner. She wants him to see it, but does not linger on the sidewalk, instead returning to the dim shadowy interior, and other tasks inside.

He keeps his *nekku* mask pulled up over the lower half of his face, as is his custom. Perhaps she of the pink parasol finds in this as much eccentricity as he finds in her umbrella.

Not a rich girl, then. Perhaps a student.

But he is forced again to reconsider when next he returns to the neighborhood. She is leaving the restaurant, mid-evening shift done. She wears stylish heels, a silky dress that skims her figure. No parasol this time. The extravagance is a raincoat, constructed smartly and fashionably of clear vinyl. She has expensive taste, individualized and fitting to her overall appearance. Money somewhere, then.

She dashes nimbly through the rain, and her scent lingers above the wet pavement. Something subtly floral, perhaps her shampoo. Cherry blossoms, or peach. His heightened senses pick it up, it is pleasing. He increases the tempo of his stride, somehow wanting to be closer to her, but she is quick, hurrying away toward other concerns, and she is long gone up the boulevard by the time he turns in toward his doorway off the avenue.

He smiles, knowing he could catch her if he wanted to, but not wanting to ruin the intrigue. Not yet. Wanting to be alone for the few moments he has earned his solitude, in a life that is not his own, has never been his own. In this place he so rarely returns to, not so much a regular neighborhood denizen because he is kept traveling and occupied elsewhere, sworn to a duty that calls him constantly away.

And so he comes infrequently from that place where he is one of many, to this place, which is his, where he can meditate, and relax, and be surrounded by the world from which he otherwise holds himself apart. Where he is simply one, an individual, even though his name is lost to memory. He cannot remember his origins either, nor can he decide whether such a loss is blessing or curse.

Pink umbrella. Or parasol. Broken this time. Trod over, bobbing uselessly in the flooded gutter, floating momentarily, as if to sail down the avenue, then dashed against the curb there that fronted his building, endlessly thwarted. Something sad and exclamatory about it that he could not name.

And then he smelled her hair. And her fear. Violence and blood. The sounds of mocking voices. He stopped short at the mouth of the alley.

There were two of them standing over her where she'd fallen, or been pushed to the ground. Her nose bloodied, her lip split and swollen. They menace, plotting their next assault, and she cringes away, trying to make herself as small as possible.

He didn't have to understand their Korean to catch the gist of it. Contempt, some sexual slight, a threat. The ineffectual hand she held up, like a surrender. *Yakuza* bullies, intoxicated, probably mean and homicidal to begin with.

Calmly, belying his inner turmoil, Roku stepped into the shadowy space between the buildings. She had ended up on the wet pavement in front of his doorway. She flinched away again, involuntarily, probably assuming he was another tormentor.

"Say that again to *me*," Roku spoke softly, but with enough authority that he was heard. Two heads turned toward his voice. One of them had a swollen jawline, and this pleased him. Cute she might be, but there was some fight in her. Retaliation had been a mistake, but the odds had not been in her favor. "Why not take up your complaint with me? Touch her again and I'll take your arms off."

"*Her?!*" Roku knew that the one who spoke first was the leader of the two. The man made a rude gesture and continued, indicating his victim with contempt. "This is no lady, and none of it is your concern, friend."

Roku approached, and he could see that her dress was ruined, torn through, exposing her undergarments, and a shape that suggested perhaps technically her assailant was correct. Evidence of male genitalia, now incompletely disguised.

Ignoring the thugs, he turned his back on them to attend her, helping her up, seeing the flash of surprise in her eyes as he gently steadied her while she climbed to her feet. He removed his dark overcoat and folded her into it, helping her lean against the wall behind her for support.

This exposed the katana which rode on his back, between his shoulderblades, and gave these orphan criminals something to think about. Without turning around, Roku looked thoughtfully at his charge while he spoke to her attackers. "Take your penis problems elsewhere."

Apparently they had some sense of self-preservation, or at least the cowardice of miscreants everywhere; they decided that challenging him might not be a wise course of action. He refused to look at them, a reminder that he did not consider them a threat, and gave the girl his full attention. They could not know how fortunate they were to be walking away, how their days were now numbered; they had started their doomsday clock. But that was for later.

And his planned retaliation was not in response to her physical injuries. He didn't need even to know her. The indignity they had visited on her affronted him. That unspoken thing that he had never been able to verbalize, his steadfast belief that the strong *should* protect the weak.

She stepped away from the wall, and perhaps did not expect the unsteadiness that she encountered. Roku looked into her bright eyes and caught her up in strong arms. He suspected, on closer inspection, that her nose was broken, and it would need attention soon. It was not troubling her yet, because adrenaline was making her shocky, protecting her from the agony of it. He knew it would be a hard fall into pain and agony once it wore off, and that would happen soon.

She pushed ineffectually against his chest, still afraid that perhaps she had just traded one peril for another. She said, her words garbled, still punch drunk, "I'm not so bad…if I can just–just…please, *leave* me be." Her tone so pitiable it made his heart hurt.

He reached out to touch her face, carefully this time, sad when she flinched yet again, so he rushed to reassure her. "No harm by my hand," he promised, stroking her cheek with the back of one finger.

This, to get her to hold still there, in the doorway, while he backtracked to the edge of the road to retrieve her parasol. Broken, but terribly cute. Too cute to abandon. Much like her, he thought, this observation coming unbidden and unavoidable to his mind.

Roku maneuvered her into the building, and was amused in an offhand way by her attempts to hide her surprise at the composed interior of his residence.

But she was starting to come down from the terror she had experienced, starting to feel the hurt and humiliation of her attack. Her clothes were ruined. The thought of her suffering made him angry and distraught; both emotions dangerous for him.

He settled her into a comfortable chair next to the efficiency kitchen before turning away to rummage briefly in the cabinets for a clean cup. Pouring a generous amount of sake, he returned to hand it to her, but she shook so terribly that he had to wrap his hands around hers to help her hold onto the cup. He gently guided it to her lips. She looked at him questioningly, so he gave a nod of reassurance, and she swallowed some of the drink, coughing a bit.

"Strong," she managed to say to him as she got herself under control. He nodded once more, unaccustomed to casual conversation.

She brought a shaky hand up to his face, touching the scars that traversed its width twice, an intrusive, curious movement that strangely did not distress him. She was still recovering from the forceful blows that had marred her face, probably slightly confused. Her attentions to his old injuries almost childlike.

He allowed this tentative exploration, and when she withdrew her fingers once more, he turned away only long enough to punch a few numbers into his phone.

Then he turned back to her, finding he was unable to take his eyes off of her face; her own searching eyes seemed to ask a million questions.

When Ichi answered his call, he apologized for the disturbance and asked if she could come immediately. He gave the address since none of his fellow priests knew it, and made two additional requests. One of which Ichi made sense of immediately, because he asked her to bring Master Go along, and she assumed Roku was injured, but the other made no sense at all, for he requested she bring a change of women's clothing.

He asked the girl's name while he rummaged in the freezer, both embarrassed and relieved when he found a small cut of *Wagyu* wrapped in butcher paper. Primitive of him, and perhaps cliché, but he gave it to her to hold against her face, hoping it would help with the swelling.

"I am Anong," she said quietly, and he could hear the distress in her voice that told him she was ready to relive her unfortunate experience in the alley.

Roku thought for a moment, trying to recall the translation. "If I recall – Anong means *'a gorgeous woman,'* right?" He thought it apt. He'd been spot on about the provenance of that parasol.

"You know Thai?" Surprise and admiration in her voice now. Perhaps distracted by the contradiction he presented her. "And what about you?" she asked, wanting to know his name.

"Roku," he told her, and something flashed in those eyes, but he was unable to read it.

"Hmmm. I bet that is not the name on your passport," she guessed, closer to the truth than she could know.

"Would it disappoint you to know that it *is* the name on my passport?" he told her, wondering what she might make of that.

"So are you in a boy band or something?" she asked, so innocently that he had to laugh. As if she could not fathom for what other reason one might call himself 'Six' and go about the world using such a moniker. She assumed it an eccentricity at best, he suspected, and at worst, a conceit. "You have the hair for it," she added, with a lopsided smile she curtailed because it hurt her, and he could see that her admiration, and the implied compliment, were sincere.

"Not even close," he assured her, shaking his head. He felt suddenly awkward, and realized he was nervous. He had no idea what to say next.

He was rescued by the muted knock at the door that alerted him to the arrival of Ichi and Go, their supernormal abilities allowing them to find him so quickly. Roku cringed slightly when introducing them, watching Anong process what he was telling her. *These are my friends, 'one' and 'five.'*

Her expression seemed to ask, *Are you serious?* What she said aloud was, "I guess it's too late for me to give you *my* code name." Again, she was mostly amused, and Roku saw that Go and Ichi recognized the humor in it, too. He reflected that the Akai were so insular that their idiosyncrasies went unnoticed amongst themselves.

"She was attacked," Roku explained, unnecessarily. "Yakuza thugs with nothing better to do." He noticed the flash of surprise in Anong's eyes at his choice of pronoun; she was touched by this simple decency. He wondered just how much she had suffered.

Go cleaned up Anong's face carefully, and shook his head at the state of her nose. "This is bad, young lady. I'll need to reset it as soon as possible. I think that lip needs at least one or two sutures as well.

"It won't be pleasant." Go was honest with her. "I have to see the tissues to get it in place, so I cannot inject it until afterward. Then I can numb it and the lip, and the rest should be easier for you. I'll also give you something for the pain before I go."

Anong nodded somberly, resigned to it. "Thank you, Doctor Five." She glanced at Roku under her lashes, and he could see that despite her little joke she was trying to master her fear.

Go placed strong, gentle fingers firmly on her face, and Roku took her hand, marveling at the delicate grip she maintained while Go made the brutal, decisive move needed to put the bones back in position. It was very quick, given his preternatural strength and skill, but Roku was unsurprised that it made Anong's eyes water terribly, having been the recipient of such a maneuver once or twice himself. She did not cry out, just took some shuddering breaths as Go administered the local anesthetic.

Then he artfully closed the gash on her lip, restoring its symmetry as well, and other than some swelling, she looked none the worse for wear. She was still shaking, though, and Roku thought that the emotional cost would be the greater.

"Beautiful forevermore," Go told her, holding her chin in his hand and looking at his handiwork. He peered more closely at the bridge of her nose. "Impossible to know for sure, but you might not even have a bump once it heals."

He excused himself then, ensuring that all understood they should call if they needed him, and left Ichi behind without a backward glance.

"I brought a few things, as I was not sure what was needed," Ichi finally spoke, patting the garment bag she had brought with her.

Roku assumed Ichi's presence would make Anong more comfortable, so he said to her, "Her clothes were ruined. She will need help in the bath."

Ichi said nothing, just looked at him as though she were seeing him for the first time. She smiled at him carefully and nodded her understanding. Roku was relieved; he could see that both of his colleagues had discerned the truth of the matter.

She turned to Anong and said, "I'm sure you're exhausted. Let's get you cleaned up so you can rest. Roku, would you make some tea while I help Anong?" The look she gave him told him she was in doubt that he had any tea at all. He shook his head at this incorrect assumption, his turn to be amused.

He turned on the teapot once the women had disappeared into the bathroom, and soon he heard water running to fill the tub. He was surprised to hear a soft knock at the door, and puzzled, went to answer.

The Collector stood in the alley beyond the bar of light that extended from the open door. Neither man spoke, when Roku stepped back in invitation, the Collector stepped forward, closing the door behind himself. Roku wondered briefly how the Collector had found the place and saved himself the trouble of asking. The man was impossibly talented at doing the impossible, and his prescience often seemed greater than that of their mistress.

"Drink?" Roku asked him.

"Thank you, no. You had some difficulty tonight?"

"A young woman was attacked. I think it a coincidence that I happened to be coming home."

"A happy coincidence, to be sure," the Collector agreed.

"I don't think it had anything to do with me, or the Mistress," Roku told him, turning to mix the matcha with the hot water, beating it carefully until it was frothy.

"And what of the victim? Is she out of danger?" the Collector asked, truly curious, and, Roku could see, genuinely concerned.

"I don't know, *Sensei*," Roku admitted readily. "I don't know her story. She works at the bistro that fronts on the next block. She must live somewhere nearby. It seemed random. It's possible they targeted her specifically, but she surprised them, so they may try to return and retaliate. I want to keep her here at least tonight, and then try to find out why it happened."

"She surprised them?" the Collector was curious. Roku thought it uncanny that the man could pick out the most significant part of what Roku had told him.

"Master Go can give you more information," Roku suggested respectfully, giving a bow. "I'd prefer not to talk about her while she is in the next room."

"Indeed," the Collector replied, and Roku could see that he understood. "I will leave you to it. Do call me if I may be of further help tonight."

"Most kind," Roku humbly thanked him, and the Collector was gone again, almost through the door before Roku finished the statement.

In a few minutes, Ichi and Anong emerged once more; fragrant steam from the bathroom followed them. Anong was composed again, she wore a flowered pink and peach kimono with a pattern not unlike her beloved umbrella. Some of her natural grace had returned, now that she was no longer exposed, and it appeared that Ichi had loosely braided Anong's long hair in some complicated style.

Her lovely face was starting to show its bruises, and she looked exhausted.

"You'll be safe here with Roku," Ichi said, looking at the other woman carefully. "I am happy to stay if that would make you feel more comfortable."

"I should go home," Anong protested, as she and Ichi accepted their green tea. "It isn't far."

"You should not be alone right now," Ichi told her. "Let us take care of you."

The young woman nodded her tentative agreement, and seemed genuinely surprised by the kindness of these strangers. Roku allowed that they must seem odd to her.

Ichi stayed close, sitting in the chair next to Anong while she finished her tea. Then she walked her over to the futon and arranged the soft bedding around Anong to make her as comfortable as possible. In just a few minutes, their charge was asleep, and Ichi returned to sit at the table with Roku.

She handed him her teacup with a knowing smile.

"Can I trust you with her?" Her question was sweet and sincere. He could not remember a time she had been this personal with him. He honestly couldn't read what the cause might be. Ichi saw his confusion and did not comment upon it; he could not yet see what she could, what Go had.

He nodded, and said nothing. He was afraid himself of what his words might betray. As Ichi stood up to leave, her hand touched his shoulder gently. She looked carefully at him a moment more, and then glanced back at the sleeping girl, thoughtfully. Another smile for herself this time, before she went back out into the night.

Roku set the locks and said his prayers, detouring into the bathroom for his own routine. He traded his clothing for soft cotton fisherman's pants and a pullover and climbed into bed with Anong, curling protectively around her, spooning with this intriguing stranger. He liked the way her body felt against his, amazed at how very different it was from his own, and he curled an arm over her carefully, and inhaled the sweet scent of her hair where it had escaped the braid and flowed across his pillow. It was enough to soothe him, enough to help him find his own sleep.

3

When Roku awoke, it was not yet dawn.

It took some restraint not to react to discovering another person in his bed, and his waking instinct was to fight, because the amnesia of sleep followed him to the surface of his consciousness.

He was gratified when this reflexive tensing did not disturb her, the events of the night before flooding back to his foggy brain, and he relaxed. While he had slept, she had turned toward him, curled into his broad chest, the top of her head below his chin, her hands against his body. She had a soft, almost ladylike snore, and this amused him.

He stretched his legs carefully and thought about how natural it felt to have her there, a surprise of sorts. He supposed it was never too late to learn something about himself, despite an unnaturally prolonged existence. He extricated himself from the covers slowly, letting her sleep, and tried to meditate, but found he was too distracted to make it through this exercise.

He showered and dressed for work, dark grey shirt, black suit. Short sword right waist, out of sight but to hand. He was tying his shoes when he noticed that she was awake, watching him.

"Good morning, Six. Time to get ready?" she inquired, and the state of her face made him angry again. The bruising had fully developed, both of her eyes ringed in purple, mouth ballooned on the left side. She saw him looking, and gamely said, "You should see the other guys."

He shook his head, but said nothing. It was a struggle to rein in his emotion about it. Her use of humor he felt was generous, and told him quite a bit about her resilience. She nodded in response and disappeared into the bath to get dressed, emerging in a cream linen shift with a princess neckline and a tailored waistline. Even Anong's ruined face couldn't diminish all the things he was responding to, beauty, spirit, grace. *All the Gods bless you, Ichi,* he said to himself, seeing the thoughtfulness she had put into choosing the clothing.

"Banker?" she guessed as she was slipping into her heels, scrutinizing his dark suit.

"Nothing so elegant," he told her. "I'm a security consultant." Then nearly grimaced, knowing how lame it sounded, considering what it really encompassed, at least in his case.

"It's okay, Dear Six, you don't have to tell me if you don't want to," Anong charmingly called him on it, putting her hand over her mouth, not quite hiding her smile.

Roku couldn't help but laugh, thinking he deserved this teasing, but whatever he would have said next was interrupted by an authoritative knock on his door. When he answered and saw Hachi standing there, gorgeous in her own impeccable black dress, his elevated mood was effectively deflated.

When any of his sisters, whether it be Ichi, Hachi, Ni, or Jūni, were dressed up, it often signaled that someone was marked for death. They took their cues from the Dragon herself. He uttered a short curse under his breath.

"I love you, too," Hachi murmured, stepping through the door, not waiting for him to invite her. She saw Anong standing there expectantly, and Roku saw Hachi's eyes widen almost imperceptibly as she made the connection. He wondered if everyone were simply quicker than he was or if she had been briefed. The latter, he decided.

They stood in awkward silence for a few long seconds, and it was Anong who spoke into the void, addressing Hachi directly. "So you must be, what – Two? Nine?"

Hachi was utterly disarmed, her sparkling laughter was genuine, and it dispelled the tension. She looked at Anong with new eyes, and then glanced at Roku with a bit of sympathy, he thought. "I *like* her. Actually, I'm *Eight*."

The two women clasped hands, and Hachi said, "You'll come with me? I will keep you safe while Roku is working." Although it sounded almost like a request, Anong could see that it wasn't. She looked at Roku for reassurance, slightly intimidated.

"I need to go home for a few things," Anong said in a smaller voice than he had heard from her before. She had great instincts, was slightly afraid.

"I will take you," Hachi said easily, relaxed and deadly as ever.

"Just for the day," Roku told Anong. "Then I will take over again." Her expression relaxed at this promise that he would see her later. She nodded and allowed Hachi to lead her away.

This was the dangerous time for Anong. There were no coincidences as far as the Akai were concerned. A damsel in distress, taking a beating in order to get close to the Dragon, and ultimately infiltrate her inner circle, was not unheard of by any means. Others had done worse, sacrificed lives in attempts to penetrate the defenses of the Akai.

No chances were ever taken, each thing had to be demonstrably proven for what it was. Or what it was not. Roku cursed himself for missing it; it was the true reason for the Collector's late-night visit. Protect Azuma and her interests at all costs.   He understood these precautions, knew well the rules of engagement, he'd enforced them himself.

He thought of the broken parasol sitting back in his empty loft and wondered if Anong might end up in similar condition.

Sending Hachi had been an unkind reminder; in many ways she *was* the best choice, he finally decided. She would not make of him a liar. He'd see Anong alive at least one more time, for good or ill, even if she were a decoy or pawn for someone else's intrigue.

It seemed every decision that Azuma made that day vexed him, rather than provide any distraction from the situation.

She seemed to balk at security precautions the most when he served as her personal guard, which perhaps should have been a compliment to his skill, or given him some measure of pride, but all he ever felt was chagrin when the Dragon was reticent to their recommendations regarding her safety. She insisted on walking through a busy downtown district rather than take the car, then made a last-minute decision to go into the *boba* shop for her tea herself.

Roku spent those ten minutes in line, facing backward, expending a menacing expression on those queueing up behind her, watching for threats. Coiled like a spring.

"Waiting for one of those schoolgirls to suddenly go rogue?" Azuma asked him archly, brows raised, far too amused at his predicament.

As he held the door for her to step back out on the sidewalk, she placed a hand on his arm as if to reassure him. Of what? There were no guarantees. Her unspoken order could end it — whatever *it* was. He'd never been in such a position. He liked it not at all. But then Azuma's brown eyes locked on his, and they were not uncaring.

Hachi, approaching him in the hotel hallway after he had dropped Azuma at the dwelling, handing the mistress off to Ku. The tiny priestess touching the small of his back, almost too soft a gesture to be noticed.

"She's clean." Hachi spoke softly, withdrawing as silently as she'd approached, and he exhaled in relief, not realizing that he had been practically holding his breath all day.

4

He discovered Anong resting in his hotel room, at the far
end of the building opposite Azuma's apartments. He
knew as soon as he unlocked the door and stepped inside.
Anong's scent, layered over the other scents of this
familiar place. Her sexy shoes cast off near the door.

This floor of the hotel was always occupied by the Akai,
the rooms never released by the hotel to outsiders. San
and Shi on either side of him. Nana, Jū, and Jūichi
opposite. The bachelor-priests.

He smiled, not at all surprised at Hachi's kindness in this
instance. He'd expected to have to seek Anong
elsewhere, but she had survived scrutiny, and Hachi had
brought her inside the fold. Had brought her to him.
Hachi had recognized how important this was to him,
intriguing as it must have been to her.

It was no less surprising to him, and he didn't pretend to
understand it.

Here, where he found himself more frequently than in
the private space he had secured.

This was the place he occupied when working, where he
had always been alone. Where he came to rest, or read,
but never in company. Unlike the others, Roku was the
most monk-like; he kept to himself. To his prayers and
meditations. Not seeking outward, peering inward. Not
elaborate nor philosophical, like Ku. Pragmatic, honed

down to the minimum necessary components required for his existence. He'd never made room for anything else.

Anong was something else. Extra.

She was stretched out atop the coverlet in the bedroom, fast asleep. Twilight just beginning outside the windows, the lights of the city like jewels starting to sparkle. Music from the bar across the avenue at street level faintly carried on the updrafts between the tall buildings, jazz piano to attract dinner guests, something soothing that would give way to more raucous karaoke later.

Roku removed his jacket and slung it over the chair, then leaned against the sill, just watching her in the soft light. After a few minutes he crossed to the bed, lying down next to her. He thought again how amazing her eyelashes were.

As if she could read his mind, but more likely as a result of the disturbance he had caused getting onto the bed, her eyes fluttered open, looking even more vulnerable with those bruises. He wanted to destroy worlds for her, finally he allowed himself the luxury of plotting his revenge.

But Anong saw this dark thing in him, recognized it, and ever so subtly reacted to it, so he shut it down, shuttering his rage, mustering a rare smile just for her. He ran a curious fingertip across her lashes, still fascinated.

"Are they yours?" he asked it before he could stop himself, at the last moment remembering how improper it must sound. This was an unspoken rule, with women, their secrets theirs, what seemed real might be fake, and it was no one's business but theirs.

To his great surprise, she laughed, not offended at all. "Yes and no. I use a serum on them at bedtime. It stimulates their growth."

"Maybe there is hope for me to make some improvements?" he asked, mock wonderingly, making a joke.

When she answered, she was all seriousness. "No. I don't think you need anything at all."

He demurred, and couldn't recall ever having such difficulty making eye contact with someone. She seemed to sense he was thinking about his scars. For the second time in as many days, she was touching them.

"You have an especially good face," she told him. "An interesting face."

He remained quiet, loving the way she touched him. Amazed that she didn't shy away from this disfigurement.

After a time, she asked, "Will you tell me how you got them?"

Not looking directly at her, he said, "I don't remember it." He looked instead at her hand on the coverlet, and picked it up in his. He ran a thumb gently across the back of her hand, and sighed. "What I know of it is secondhand."

She said nothing, waiting for him to decide, giving him an opportunity to deflect, or change the subject, and he knew she would be content with his decision, whatever it was. Which made talking about it easier, or perhaps he felt she could understand.

"I was just a baby when it happened," he told her. "On the market road through the mountains a man accosted my mother. He didn't want her to be conflicted about her response to the chaos he was creating, so he sought to eliminate the source of her resistance, her child. He took his scythe to me, no hesitation, and discarded me at the roadside. That took all the fight out of her, and he made off with her in her grief.

"But I lived. I was rescued. If his blows had been higher, my infant skull would have given way, any lower, I would have been decapitated."

"And your father?" she asked, thinking the story had a happy ending.

He shrugged. "I have no knowledge of him. A monk who witnessed the violence took me in."

"The monk became your family, then? You were cared for?" she asked, seeming relieved.

He was so quiet that she knew it had not been a happy alternative. "My childhood was…pragmatic. I endured it, participated in temple life. The monks taught us to survive. They were the keepers of my story, they told me the cause of my scarring."

And taught me how to seek retribution, he thought.

"And love?" Anong prompted him, reading the heart of the matter, thinking she was beginning to understand his unusual name, the names of his colleagues.

"An unattainable luxury. Reserved for others. My honor lies in service. In the protection I provide."

"To whom? The Emperor?" Anong was only half-joking, understanding that her use of humor was a calculated defense, necessitated by her real fear about who he might be. She had realized that he, along with the others, was part of a very elite group.

She had watched him turn his back on those very dangerous orphans of the Yakuza, had seen her assailants withdraw from him, when they should have killed him just for daring to interrupt. And finished with her. She was both curious about his secrets and desirous of keeping them.

"Someone even more important," he told her, and something in his bearing betrayed more emotion than he wanted to, because Anong saw, finally, what she had been searching for.

"Ah. A personal devotion, but not a lover," she aptly concluded. Her eyes searched his for confirmation.

"Indeed. She saved me."

"From that life?" Anong wondered.

"From the monster I had become," he admitted, and in that statement Anong thought she detected some shame.

Roku propped his head on his hand and looked at Anong carefully. His expression told her he had no desire to say more. "And you?"

"What do you want to know?" she asked.

Everything, he thought, but said only, "You can tell me about you."

"You've already forced me to admit the regrettable truth about my eyelashes," she said, hoping he would understand that she just wasn't ready to make herself any more vulnerable than she already was. He knew the essential secret about her, which wasn't truly a secret, and that hadn't seemed to spook him. It had been a long time since a man had been genuinely interested in who she was.

"Then about the men who attacked you, perhaps," he suggested gently.

"I don't know them," she said, too quickly, something flickering in her eyes. A lie? She saw him recognize it, and rushed to explain. "Not really, anyway. They come into the restaurant now and then."

"To see you?" His question both genuinely curious, understanding such a motivation, and he was surprised at what else his tone conveyed. Jealousy.

She smiled. "I don't know. To drink, mostly. I don't think their interest is specific to me; that would require some kind of humanity. I think those two are merely creatures of appetite."

Her mouth twisted with revulsion, and she could no longer maintain eye contact. Roku felt the goosebumps rising on her skin. He said nothing, waited on her to continue, not wanting to be a source of further suffering, and ran gentle hands along her arms to warm her.

But perhaps he had underestimated her resolve, and her courage. Bravely, she added, "They followed me when I left work that night. I suspect they wanted to take their pleasure of me by force, and then got something they hadn't bargained for, didn't expect. It made them even uglier."

"And do they come into the restaurant on a certain night, or with other people?" he asked, thinking he was being subtle.

"Sometimes with others not unlike them," Anong allowed, thinking. "I know what they are. The owner seems to defer to them, not out of any motivation other than fear."

"Which is probably a healthy response," Roku said.

"And is your response going to be similarly so?" Anong wisely saw where his inquiries were leading. "Leave it alone. I recognize you do not fear them, perhaps would even pursue them."

"Critical lessons burn in the learning." Roku's mouth set in a hard line. She softened it by placing her finger on it.

"I...feel sorry for them," Anong concluded simply. "As I understand it, they are orphans, and for that reason they are targeted by the clans. They have nowhere else to go, no options other than lawlessness. It becomes the family they are looking for."

Still, Roku cannot stand the insult. He tries to explain it to her, but she shakes her head. She understands him, but disagrees.

"I know who I am. No one else can tell me something so fundamental unless I let them. No one else defines me. And I cannot give anyone that power over me.

"A second insult cannot erase the first. They know no other life, have not the capacity to behave any better, and I am guessing that you do," Anong spoke softly, and gave him the full measure of her gaze. He felt he could drown in the depths of it. And then a plea. "I hope I shall not be proved wrong about you."

With one statement, he knew any retaliation he planned against them would not be sanctioned by her. A surprise. But he thought her wrong; he lived as he always had, by the sword, and the code that governed it. And here she was, the victim, not so gently directing him along another path.

"Are you hungry?" he asked then, letting go of the subject with a lopsided smile. "Let me feed you and then I will take you home."

He read her pleasure that he would be spending more time with her, and perhaps her relief that there did not seem to be any other immediate expectations.

Roku purposefully avoided asking about the report that had been compiled on Anong; normally he would have been curious for such details. In this case, he truly wanted to learn about her the old-fashioned way. And he wanted to be able to be honest that he had not been a party to the background check, not that he suspected she would ever find out about their probing.

Anong was surprised at his chivalry; when she alerted her employer to request a few days off, he informed her that someone had already dropped in to tell him about her attack.

He had an uncanny way of anticipating when she got caught in the rain with heavy bags of groceries. After her face healed, and she went back to work, there was always a car hired to take her safely home after a late shift. On rare occasions, he showed up himself to escort her.

Then there were the nights he showed up at her apartment, late. Always he messaged her first, unfailingly considerate. No words, just the number – '6.' She sent back emojis. If chopsticks, he brought food. A microphone if she was out hosting a party. A cocktail if she were still at work, in which case he would show up after closing to take her elsewhere for a quiet drink.

Never a pattern. Nights such as those few and far between, not because she suspected he had someone else, but because of the demands of providing protection. His life was more than that, she knew, but never asked.

If she replied with a 'Zzz,' he knew she had been asleep. She had sent it that first time regretfully, knowing she saw so little of him. But he had shown up anyway, directing her back to bed when she came to answer the door, curling his body against her atop the fluffy *shikibuton*. Her own sleeping guardian, never pressing any advantage.

She gave him a key, finally, and he seemed pleased that he would not have to wake her up. He recognized that it was her admission that she had no one else, that he was never going to walk in and discover her with another man. He didn't tell her that he didn't need a key to get into anything.

Despite this, he never came without sending that '6' ahead of time. On one of those rare occasions she had been too tired to wait up, she had awakened to the sound of the shower running in the early hours, before he joined her.

Anong reached a point where she would answer with 'Zzz' even if she had other plans, just to have an excuse to leave a party, or beg off getting drinks with friends after work, more interested in being alone with him. He was onto her then, too.

"We never go out," he teased her in mock protest. "I worry that you don't want to be seen with me."

"I don't want to share you, Six," she told him, and he could see that she was only half kidding.

"What if I want to show you off?" he asked. "Just standing next to you improves my reputation."

"Let's go then, Tokyo is open all night, I'll just get dressed," she had laughed, actually throwing the covers off the bed. "I'll go anywhere with you."

But he had tugged on her arm, pulling her back down into his embrace, tracing her eyebrows with gentle fingers.

"Not necessarily *now*."

Roku never left anything behind, when he was gone, he was gone. No stray socks, no keys, no forgetting his phone. No part of him stayed with her, except his scent on her sheets. The phantom memory of his touch. The whisper of secrets that he kept from her, secrets that she suspected he must keep at all costs.

Anong wondered if he were a celibate. Tried to calm her own insecurity about the reasons for it. It seemed to be unrelated to the reality of her state of being; he was genuinely unconflicted and unambiguous about his feelings for her.

Even for one so quiet, some responses can neither be manufactured nor hidden. Especially those that signal male desire. Months passed, but he never made any move to undress her. Just held her in his arms as they slept.

Until the night she answered his text with a toothbrush, implying that he might need to keep one around. He teased her about it, as usual, deflecting.

"Was that a hint about my breath?" he asked, hanging his jacket over a chair and unbuttoning his shirtsleeves to roll them back. "Or because you want me to stop using yours?" he asked, with his characteristic mischief. Anong did not know that what she saw in him he hid from everyone else.

"I just thought you should be able to make yourself at home," Anong told him, and her eyes were smiling but she curled her legs up under her on the couch, betraying her fear of rejection. "Keep your *own* toothbrush here?"

"Ah." He nodded, but said nothing further as he sat down next to her, and leaned in close. He understood the toothbrush was a metaphor for something else, a commitment of sorts, a claiming.

As usual, he let his actions speak, more clearly than before. He slid warm strong hands into her hair, cradling her face, his watch cool and smooth against her jaw. He held her like that for a few moments, his own face mere centimeters away, his eyes searching hers. Then his mouth closed over hers, tongue probing, gentle at first and then more insistent, until she was breathless with want, and he'd made his point. He put her in her bed and was not hesitant when he touched her, all of her, and she realized his reluctance had been simply that of one who was inexperienced. His sweetness overwhelmed her, and he made it abundantly clear just what she meant to him.

That night she told him her story. About life in rural Phang Nga, growing up so different from everyone else. She had been the only boy in the family, which made her important to continuing the family name.

But if there were tragedy in her life, it had not been there. Surprisingly, her father had understood her, had accepted her. Which forced the other members of their small fishing village to do the same.

She swam every day in the sparkling Andaman Sea, pretending she was a mermaid. And she did everything she was asked to do, she was a dutiful son, but she knew that she could not stay there. Knew that her happiness, her fulfillment, could only be found in seeking a way to be truly herself. And that could only happen elsewhere.

She told him of the fisherman father who gave her another name, made her Anong, as was his right to do. Recognized her anew as a daughter before she left for Krung Thep. Gifted her a pink parasol.

Then, in the city, how so many like her turned to the sex trades to survive, to honor their obligations to support family back home. Survived discrimination, were ostracized, sometimes beaten, all too often to death. Just for being ladyboys.

How she had refused to succumb to despair, learning, working hard, eventually noticed by others for her unique style. Sought by promoters who needed a pretty face to host a club opening, or a party. Discovered by one that was honest, that gave her a chance to be a star, brought her to Japan to host at a new club, absent the physical obligations that were all too often imposed upon her sisters.

From there, a work visa, the job at *Belle*'s. More money than she had ever known. Legitimate.

It had brought her to him. And he knew why. She was his. More importantly, and more frightening to Roku, he was hers.

6

In the bathhouse at the stronghold, with Ku, after a grueling session in the dojo, Roku floated lazily in the warm water.

"How is she? Your friend," Ku inquired, surprising Roku with the question.

"She is well. Recovered, at least physically," Roku told him. But Ku stayed silent. He probably had the most to say of all his fellow priests, but Roku appreciated that when Ku said something, it was always meaningful. No wasted speech.

Roku surprised both himself and Ku when he spoke again almost immediately. "She makes me feel like I'm not myself anymore – or who I thought I was…"

"Stop resisting," Ku advised. "That feeling has a name." Ku's smile inscrutable, ever the philosopher.

"It's just, I never realized that I was-" Roku began, but Ku didn't let him finish.

"You're not a tin of sardines; you need not label it. I'm not sure the words we use have anything to do with love. It's too great a thing to be bound by small ideas.

"Anong is a woman. Anatomy might restrict us physically, but emotionally, mentally, we can be truly free. She has escaped an essential boundary. Probably an unnecessary one. Are you so blind to the example of that freedom that you live with every day? That we have known since we left the Temple?"

The Mistress. The Dragon. Azuma defied and expanded definition, and Roku wondered if it was his life with her that had made him open to the possibility presented by Anong.

"It isn't really a conundrum, my friend," Roku clarified. He reached out a hand toward Ku, who grasped and squeezed it. It felt good to be understood. "She calms me; I love nothing more than to settle next to her and bury my face in her hair. I feel when I am with her that it is the only time I can truly rest."

"We are both fortunate in this," Ku agreed, and Roku was surprised at this public acknowledgement of his intimacy with Hachi. "Not for us the fate of our brothers San and Shi, who have subverted their humanity to satisfy their greater appetites."

Roku nodded, though he had often wondered whether the existence of his brother priests was the more honest. Eliciting terror and pain to savor the blood had appealed to him initially as well, because strong emotion flavored its taste, heightened the experience, fed the monster. The anguish had always disturbed him; he was intelligent enough to understand that it was probably an aftereffect, the echo in his memory of his mother's screams.

Roku had learned, in a moment of weakness, that pleasure and desire seasoned the blood just as much, and since then he had used other means to obtain gratification in feeding.

"Perhaps you are the more fortunate, as you do not have to seek sustenance outside your primary relationship," Ku observed wisely.

Roku made a face, which surprised Ku. "She doesn't know. I think I am afraid to show her the ugliness because I cannot offer her what is not mine to give."

"When we lie to someone we love," Ku responded, "we are really only lying to ourselves. It is a near certainty that she already knows your essential truth, if not the shape and the details of it."

"I can never belong to her," Roku protested.

"Never? What a strange word to use. It is evident that a part of you already does. Take care not to miss out on what you have now in favor of concerns about what may never be." Damnable Ku. Correct, as always.

"Yet it is unfair to her to promise something I do not have–" Roku insisted, unsure why he was so ready to argue.

"My friend, do not put off anything of importance for the future you are not promised," Ku advised wisely.

"Should not the death I am promised keep me from inviting her love?" Roku had thought he was doing Anong a kindness by keeping her from it. "Have I not already been cruel and selfish for giving her some belief of it?"

Ku's eyes betrayed his surprise and his sadness that Roku had missed an essential lesson. One that he, the philosopher, had always espoused, from the time before he had escaped the Temple of Akenomyosei. "Death is not to be feared. It is to be embraced, like an old friend. A friend who reminds us to live — as fully as ever we can."

7

Roku struggles.

Anong sees him brooding, wanting to let go of something. "What haunts you so?" The question interrupts a quiet evening.

"I feel you have sacrificed much of what you would do in deference, in waiting, for me," he admitted reluctantly.

"Perhaps you do not see that every choice you have made from the very first moment we met only served to support my definition of who I am. I give up nothing to be with you, unless it is disappointment," Anong replied. "You made that part of it important. That's the kind of respect we all hope for, and so many of us never find. And I am talking about everyone, not just a marginalized group. How hard it is to find someone willing to love us as we are. I am spoiled with you."

"Yet I cannot give you more than this, and I think you deserve so much more." Roku wanted to make her understand. He could not see what she did, that he was afraid for her, and it made him push her away.

"I could trade what I have found with you for someone who could take me to the beach, spend more time, spend more anything, but it is not quantity that transforms a thing, makes it profound where it was formerly common. It is the quality of that thing, and quality is not readily found. I would dishonor the incandescent beauty of what we have to complain. I have more than many ever will."

"That kind of scale will never balance, will it?" he asked, and she was surprised by the bitterness in his tone. She understood his defensiveness as a way of deflecting the depth of what he was feeling, and perhaps some guilt.

"The scales were never going to balance, no matter what, and I accept that. Instead of focusing on the subtractions, I would rather celebrate the additions." She touched his face gently. "You can do that, can't you?"

He loved her optimism.

But he was a pragmatist who knew that the additions she referred to were liabilities in his world. And the subtractions he faced there could prove deadly.

For all that Anong wanted Roku to forget, there were others who remembered. Others not so generous in their view of the situation. Those who found Anong's very existence an insult.

Cowards do not retaliate against strength. Not against that strength that they did not challenge when it first presented to them. They find weakness, and exploit it.

Roku was late to meet her in the lobby of the hotel, the one she jokingly referred to as his, so she went into the bar for a drink, innocently sure he would not be long. The tall windows afforded a view of the lounge from both the street and the lobby.

Unlike Roku, she was less aware of her surroundings and the people in it. By the time she noticed the two men staring at her from the opposite side of the bar, and recognized them, it would have been impossible to escape them.

Their expressions belied their intent, and they had every reason to be confident. She was alone. She avoided eye contact, but could tell by the tone of their conversation that she was the subject. They had not forgotten their thwarted attack; they had merely been lying in wait for a time when they could see their plans through to a sadistic conclusion.

Initially, she had her own reasons to be confident, her own protection coming. But a quarter hour later and no sign of him. A glance at her watch worried her more. Roku was never late.

The more dominant of the pair across from her suddenly put out his cigarette and got to his feet. His partner mirrored him, and the two of them split up, each coming around the bar from separate directions, making it impossible for her to avoid them, even if she were foolish enough to leave the safety of this public place. She knew that men like these could take her from here, bodily, and whether she went silently or screaming, the other patrons of the hotel would conveniently not see a thing, out of fear of being targeted by one of the clans, being made to disappear as she could be made to disappear. Her fear was a living thing.

One of the men seated himself on her left, and leaned in close enough that she felt his breath on her hair. As the other approached from the right, the bartender turned away, and Anong despaired that she would have any help. But just as quickly, he turned back, with a glass of sparkling wine that he placed to her right. His calm, level gaze was directed at another person behind her, to whom he nodded, clearly deferent to this patron for whom the drink was intended.

Anong found the courage to glance to the right, and saw that her second assailant appeared to have come to a halt several feet away, the expression on his face unreadable.

"Thank you, Ohno." A woman's cultured voice spoke, ahead of the manicured hand that reached for the wineglass and picked it up. Every hair on Anong's body was suddenly standing on end.

Anong half-turned, thinking this interruption had possibly saved her, and was surprised to see an extremely tall, impossibly lovely woman in a sharply tailored dress standing very close to her. The woman looked thoughtfully at the man to Anong's left, and ignored the one to the right.

"You are in my seat," the woman spoke to the man calmly, but Anong recognized something dangerous in her tone. In response, the man scrambled off the barstool and stood up, moving a few feet away, betraying obvious fear.

The second man displayed some false bravado as he resumed his approach from the right, but the woman spoke dismissively to him as well, saying, as she settled to Anong's left, "That seat is mine, too."

Rather than respond, he gave her a sly expression, and it telegraphed a challenge as he settled instead on the next stool but one. Still close to Anong, but not to her immediate right.

The young man's partner still clearly wanted no quarrel with the woman, and he remained at a slight remove, looking very much afraid and as though he might actually flee.

"I apologize, sir, but all of the seats in this bar belong to Dr. Himura, and since you have demonstrated your hostility toward her, I must ask you to leave." Ohno spoke softly from behind the bar. Anong noticed for the first time how intimidating he was, something she had not picked up on before.

The woman then did something very curious. She placed a hand on the small of Anong's back and leaned in close. Anong flinched, unsure whether this was to be another assault, but the woman merely whispered, "Play along." She sounded amused, delighted even, as though it were all a bit of fun.

The man to the right stood up as slowly as he dared, and spoke insolently to his friend. Anong tried to pick out a word or two, but the only word she did identify did not make any sense.

When the woman saw that her message had been received, she pulled away, removing her hand from Anong's back. She sipped her wine quietly for a few more moments, waiting for the men to leave, which, after a reluctant argument, they did. Then she stayed a bit longer, staring contemplatively off into the distance, and eventually her eyes widened slightly, as though she heard a sound that only she could hear. Finally, she placed a reassuring hand over Anong's, briefly, before she departed, just as suddenly as she had come, taking her wine and disappearing into the lobby.

A moment later, Roku was there, and Anong realized that she had been holding her breath. She sighed it out in relief, still not understanding what had happened, what it all meant.

"They won't be bothering you again," Ohno observed, with a satisfied smile. He placed a bottle of Kirin Select on the bar next to a clean tumbler.

"*Origato, Ohno-San,*" Roku said, taking the seat the woman had abandoned. To Anong, when Ohno had turned to other tasks, he added, "It's over."

"What is?" Anong was confused. "You're late." She let her exasperation be heard, and was immediately sorry. She had been afraid, but it wasn't his fault. She had restrained whatever he had originally wanted to do to those men.

"My boss. She doesn't say much, but the clans won't dare interfere with you again." Roku sipped his beer, and even he was faintly smiling. Anong knew he was fond of his employer, knew she was important, but she still couldn't understand why both Ohno and Roku were so certain.

"How can you know?" she wondered aloud.

"Once the Dragon acknowledges you, her protection extends to you," Roku explained.

"I don't understand," Anong said, looking to him for answers.

"You asked me for restraint," he said. "She made me late. It was the least she could do. Even if you don't understand, they do. They recognized their last chance to leave with their lives, and they took it."

"She doesn't even know me," Anong protested.

"You asked me once if I had known love," Roku reminded her. "That is her version of it. She takes care of her own. You are important to me, by extension you are important to her. And I get to keep my promise to my girlfriend that I will try not to kill assholes that mess with her."

"Six, that is one of the nicest things anyone has ever said to me, but it isn't an answer." Anong was still trying to understand.

It was Ohno who spoke up before Roku had a response.

"Well, you're cute."

"Ridiculous," Anong said, looking from the bartender to Roku and back. She was trying hard to discover whether they were teasing, but they looked perfectly serious.

Roku shook his head, thinking about the very first time he had seen her. How she had changed him. "Never underestimate the power of cuteness."

Author's Note

Special thanks this time to Lynell Ingram for cover design. She elevated my pedestrian artwork, transforming it from idea into vision. But that's what Lynell does – she elevates everything she touches.

The novella that anchors this collection of short stories, *Duet des Fleurs*, was composed and written in three days. Yes, seventy-two hours. Stacy-the-Great got the mad idea that we should participate in the International 3-Day Novel Contest held every year over Labor Day weekend, since we were in the throes of COVID, and no one had any better plans. The premise is just what you'd imagine. From Friday midnight through Monday midnight you must write a complete, not necessarily coherent, reasonably edited composition and submit your work to get a certificate for your (not insignificant) pains. This is what I came up with under duress. Each morning beginning with optimism, and by 6 pm each evening convinced that I was building a snowman out of…well, poop. Ultimately, I was proud I finished. Some things are great just because you can say you did them. I have a feeling I might have to try this again sometime, albeit NOT soon.

The other stories were written for short-story month, May 2021.

The first is my paltry tribute to the amazing Oliver Sacks. I loved reading about his patients, and I loved his talent for writing through humor and grief with equal facility.

Of course, in my case, said homage dealt with a macabre, almost Hitchcockian, scenario.

Then a bit of flash fiction about a Devil's meeting, and a girl who puts one over on the Lord of the Underworld. An odd marriage of prose and poetry; an attempt at something different. I cannot say I was stepping out of my comfort zone, this of all the work presented here is a true distraction. It took the longest to write, the longest to master, and I hope you will stare at it until you see the pattern.

Next, Commander Vega's story is actually just the beginning of a much longer saga. I think. As always, I am probably overpromising and underdelivering, because I do not have a timeline as to when we will next encounter our intrepid hero and the fascinating artificial intellect that is *Sagittarius*.

Finally, a *fourth* story came to me at the eleventh hour, and I have included it here. A voice from the void spoke loudly in my ear with only ten days left in the month of May.

I always wondered about the scars on Roku's face, but he never talked about them, so it would have been terribly impolite of me to ask. I never wrote about them either, somehow feeling that their description would invite unwanted inquiries, questions I was unable and unwilling to answer. He could see that I was curious but perhaps too kind, and I admit, too timid (Roku is both scary and intimidating) to ask. So I was surprised when he started to tell me about his past, and delighted when he entrusted me with the story of how he met Anong. And I think he wanted that backstory told before I wrote a book about the *Akai*. (Thank you, Elizabeth, for forbearance.)

The Thai people recognize a third gender, those known colloquially as ladyboys. These women take hormones and often have breast augmentation surgeries. Far less frequently do they undergo completion gender reassignment surgery. Because it is honorable within that culture for young people to support their relatives, and due to significant workforce discrimination, an unfortunate number of these women are forced to do sex work to provide for themselves and for their families.

There exists overwhelming evidence of self-reported heterosexual men who share lifelong relationships with these women, a fact which supports gender fluidity as a natural function of human sexuality and sexual expression. Love is love, and I agree wholeheartedly with Ku: it refuses to conform to small ideas.

About the Author

LJ Farrow is absolutely convinced she needs some sort of professional help. She resides in rural Indiana alongside three geniuses and a small but determined *Erinaceus concolor.*